ARIES I

THE KING OF MARS

JEREMY D SCHOLZ

For information or permission requests, contact:

Jeremy D Scholz

https://jeremydscholz.com/

ISBN: 979-8-9994313-5-6

Printed in the United States of America

First Edition

Aries I – The King of Mars

by Jeremy D Scholz

jeremydscholz.com

To my seventh-grade scientists, explorers, and dreamers.
You imagined what life on Mars could be like
and dared to build it in your minds.
Every time you asked a question,
designed a habitat,
or solved a problem no one had faced before,
you brought that distant red world a little closer.

This book is for you
for your curiosity, your courage,
and your belief that the future belongs
to those brave enough to dream beyond Earth.

INTRODUCTION

For centuries, humankind has stared at the red glow in the night sky and called it Mars,

a symbol of war, of mystery, of the unreachable.

But what if it wasn't unreachable?

What if it was destiny?

Aries I – The King of Mars begins where humanity's greatest dream collides with its deepest fears. It's the story of a mission that dares to build a home on another world, and the people whose hearts must cross the distance long before their bodies ever do.

Within the silence of space and the dust of a new frontier, legends are not born, they are built, one breath, one decision, one sacrifice at a time.

This is not just the story of going to Mars.

It is the story of what it means to stay there...
and what it costs to call a new world home.

J.S.

The Red Dream

Commander Noah Karalis had always believed in impossible things.

He believed in stars you couldn't see yet, in landscapes that hadn't been walked, and in the idea that one day, humankind would thrive on a red planet millions of miles from Earth. While other kids were dreaming of becoming astronauts, Noah was already sketching habitat domes in his notebook margins and calculating oxygen ratios.

By twenty-eight, he was the youngest propulsion engineer NASA had ever promoted to director-level status. By thirty-nine, he had designed the engine that would take the first colonists to Mars. But he didn't just want to send them. He wanted to go. And he wanted to stay there.

It became his life's purpose: not just to explore Mars, but to make it home.

When a private company with the same vision offered him the opportunity to command the first party of colonists, he jumped at it. He had been training ever since.

When his son was born, there was never a moment of doubt. The boy would be called Aries, after the god of war, after the first sign of the zodiac, and, of course, after the planet Mars itself.

"Welcome to the world, Aries," Noah whispered into the newborn's ear, his voice breaking with emotion. "You're already part of something bigger than either of us."

Aries Karalis was brilliant from the beginning. He solved puzzles before he could talk, recited orbital mechanics before kindergarten, and argued with his teachers by first grade, politely, but convincingly. He had his father's mind, sharp as a laser, and twice as fast.

But he was still a kid.

And kids, no matter how brilliant, get bored. They sneak cookies from the nutrition lab, reprogram cleaning bots to stage fake alien attacks, and sometimes, just sometimes, they get into far more trouble than anyone expects.

Especially when they're growing up in the shadow of a dream the size of a planet.

This is the story of a father who dared to chase the stars, and a son who had to find his own place among them.

Before Mars became their home, it was their destiny.

1

LIFE'S NOT FAIR

The rain began just after midnight, soft at first, like fingertips drumming gently on glass. Tap-tap-tap. A hesitant rhythm. Then came the wind, low and moaning through the eaves, as if the sky itself was bracing for something it couldn't stop.

Aries lay cocooned beneath two heavy quilts, trembling. His head throbbed as if someone had stuffed it with hot sand; his throat scraped raw from hours of coughing. Each hack rattled his chest, clawing up from somewhere deep, deeper than lungs. It hurt. His eyes watered, his skin slick with fever-sweat.

The bottle of cough syrup was empty on the kitchen counter.

"I'll be back in fifteen minutes," Mom had said, brushing his damp hair away from his burning forehead. Her palm was cool, her touch light, like she was trying not to wake something fragile. She smiled a brave, ordinary smile and kissed his cheek, quick and warm.

She tucked a small stuffed bear under his arm. "Here, he will comfort you." It was a prize he had won in a claw game. He had given it to her last Mother's Day. She reached for the doorknob.

"Just some medicine," she said. "Just down the road."

She wrapped herself in her coat, the zipper catching halfway. Rain hit the roof harder now. He heard the screen door bang once, then again. Her keys jingled. The car engine turned over, then faded into the storm.

Aries dragged himself out of bed and pressed his face to the cold window. He watched the red blur of her taillights melt into the night, swallowed by the rain.

He waited.

The storm worsened, snarling against the windows, shaking the old walls. Time stretched out; waiting became unsettling. Still no sound of tires on the drive. No creak of the front door. Just the groan of wind, and his own cough, growing hoarser.

At some point he must've dozed off, because the next thing he knew, the sky outside was pale with morning.

And the front door still hadn't opened.

The medicine bottle sat where it had hours ago, hollow, and useless.

He curled up on the kitchen floor, wrapped in a blanket that smelled like her. The clock ticked too loudly. The silence filled the rest.

He tried not to cry.

He tried not to be afraid.

He failed.

When the door finally swung open, it was hours later. Aries leapt up, heart sprinting.

"Mom..."

But it wasn't her.

Commander Noah Karalis stepped in, shoulders broad in his dark uniform, the knees of his pants crusted with red brick dust meant to simulate Mars. His boots left a trail of it across the carpet. Mom would've scolded him for that.

Aries froze.

His father's eyes were hollow, bloodshot. He didn't say anything at first. Just looked at his son, then slowly, painfully, knelt to his level. Like gravity had gotten heavier.

Aries knew something was wrong. He felt it in his chest before the words came.

"Where's Mom?"

Noah opened his mouth, but nothing came out. His jaw clenched. His face crumpled.

"There was... an accident," he whispered at last, like it physically hurt to say. "Last night. On her way back from the pharmacy."

The words hung in the air like smoke, thick and choking.

"No..." Aries shook his head. "No, she said...she said she'd be back. She promised. Fifteen minutes."

"I know," Noah said, broken. "I know, son."

"I *need* her," Aries choked. His voice cracked, shattered.

Noah reached for him, arms steady, strong, but Aries didn't move. Didn't lift his own arms. Didn't feel the hug. He stood stiff in his father's grasp, numb.

He couldn't breathe.

He couldn't scream.

So he just stood there, hollow and shaking, as something inside him, something warm and bright and necessary, cracked down the middle.

That night, the house was quiet in a different way. Not peaceful.

Empty.

The sound of her footsteps, her laughter, her humming in the kitchen — gone.

And buried beneath that silence, beneath blankets and fever and the smell of rain on pavement, a part of Aries Karalis, the part that believed the world was safe, that promises always came true, was lost.

She went out because of him.

And never came back.

ULTIMATUM

The rain had stopped, but Noah Karalis still heard it, phantom droplets ticking across the windshield, even though the vehicle's glass was dry.

He sat motionless in the loading bay parking lot of the Mars Expedition Headquarters, hands gripping the wheel of his company-issued vehicle, though the engine had long since gone cold. Outside, the world looked washed out. Pale clouds smeared the sky. Inside, the silence was suffocating.

The passenger seat was empty, which made a lump form in his throat.

He'd kept glancing toward it during the drive, out of habit. Expecting her voice, her fingers brushing his wrist as she adjusted the heating dial or scolded him about forgetting breakfast again. But there was only a child's jacket tossed over the seat, and the empty echo of what used to be.

Noah hadn't cried when they called him. Not at first. Not when they said the word collision or fatal. Not when he arrived at the crash site and saw the shattered glass and broken frame and the stupid bottle of cough medicine still crumpled in a paper bag on the passenger floor.

He hadn't cried when he told Aries.

But now, parked beneath the headquarters that held his life's work, his mission, his future, he wanted to scream.

He ran a hand over his jaw, felt the roughness of three-day stubble. He had gone from command simulations to planning a funeral in less than twenty-four hours. From orbit insertion briefings to explaining death to his son. He didn't know how to live in both worlds.

He couldn't. Not anymore.

Mars was supposed to be a new beginning. Not an escape.

Aries hadn't cried either, not at first. Noah had held him, but the boy's arms had hung limp, and his eyes had just stared forward, blank. It was the kind of silence that didn't belong in a child. The kind that settled deep, like frost in the bones.

Noah exhaled slowly and stepped out of the car. The shuttle doors hissed shut behind him as he walked toward the main building, his boots tracking Martian simulation dust across the polished concrete. He didn't brush it off.

The elevator ride was too quiet. His reflection stared back at him in the mirrored wall: square shoulders, sharp uniform, eyes rimmed with exhaustion. The face of the man chosen to lead the most ambitious colonization effort in human history.

And the face of a man who had just buried his wife.

He paused outside the conference room. Through the glass, Earth rotated slowly in its projected orbit above the table, so blue, so whole. So far away from everything that hurt.

Noah squared his shoulders and stepped inside.

"Commander Karalis," Director Erick Caulder said, standing to greet him. "We appreciate your punctuality."

Noah nodded stiffly. "I didn't come here for pleasantries, Director."

Caulder gestured to the seat at the end of the long table. "Then let's begin."

They were alone, save for Dr. Laney Sierra, the mission psychologist, perched quietly at the edge of the room with her tablet. Her eyes followed everything.

Noah remained standing.

"You're asking me to leave my son behind," he said, voice low but firm. "I won't do that."

Caulder didn't blink. "With respect, Commander, this isn't your personal expedition. This mission is humanity's first permanent outpost on another planet. It is not a daycare. We cannot, will not, jeopardize it."

"He's not a passenger. He's part of the team."

"He's ten."

"He's *brilliant*," Noah snapped. "His cognitive scores are higher than every one of your flight engineers. He helped debug the habitat AI last fall, caught a line of logic recursion even our lead programmer missed."

"That may be true," Caulder said coolly, "but psychological resilience and social maturity are not measured by IQ."

Noah stepped forward, his voice trembling now, not with anger, but with something deeper. "You want to talk about psychology? Then understand this: Aries has no one. No grandparents. No relatives we trust. His mother is *gone*, and I wasn't there. I was running oxygen collapse drills while she bled out in the rain for cough medicine. For our son."

The room went still.

Caulder's mouth pressed into a line. Even Dr. Sierra looked down, for just a moment.

"I failed her," Noah whispered. "And I will not fail him. You want me on that mission? Then he comes with me. Otherwise..." he swallowed hard. "Find another commander."

Caulder sighed. "You know we don't have another you."

"Then don't ask me to be less than human."

Caulder glanced toward Dr. Sierra, whose expression remained unreadable. Then she turned back to Noah, folding her hands on the table.

"He'd have to pass every psychological and physical benchmark. Five years of accelerated training with only three years to complete it. Simulations. Isolation chambers. Gravity adjustments."

"He can do it."

"And if he doesn't?"

"He will," Noah said again, this time more softly, more desperately.

Caulder's face was impassive. "You realize what this does to our risk profile. To optics. To funding."

"You want optics?" Noah said, stepping closer. "Try this: humanity begins again on Mars, and a father gets to raise his son. You think donors won't rally behind that?"

Caulder's silence was not disagreement.

"I'm not asking for favors," Noah said. "I'm giving you everything I have. Every piece of me that's left. But I won't leave him here to grow up without either of his parents."

Caulder looked again at Dr. Sierra. This time, the psychologist gave a small nod.

The director stood, slow and deliberate. His voice lost its sharpness, softened by something older than protocol.

"You were her friend, too," Noah said quietly.

"I was." Dr. Sierra affirmed.

"Then you know she'd want him with me."

Caulder studied him a moment longer. Then finally... he spoke.

"He completes the full program. No shortcuts. No special allowances."

"Agreed."

"If he falters..." Caulder probed.

"He won't."

Caulder nodded once. "Then we're done here."

Noah started to breathe a little more assured. His shoulders slumped just a little.

"He's on the manifest," Caulder added. "Wave One. Aries Karalis, age ten."

Noah looked down at his hands. They were shaking.

Dr. Serria's tone changed, quieter now. "For what it's worth, I think she'd be proud."

Noah didn't answer. His voice had gone somewhere he couldn't reach.

As he left the room, the Earth projection still spun above the table, serene, detached.

But deep inside Commander Noah Karalis, amid the guilt, the grief, and the unspoken weight of all he'd lost, there was the faintest flicker of purpose again.

Aries wouldn't be left behind.

They were going to Mars.

Together.

3

THE GAUNTLET

T he shuttle hissed as its doors released, and a blast of Sonoran heat slammed into the cabin like the breath of a sleeping dragon awakened. Aries Karalis, ten years old and brimming with restless energy, stepped out behind his father, blinking into the hard white glare of the desert sun.

His boots crunched on red-dusted gravel, and his mouth fell open.

Before him stretched a sprawl of domes, satellite towers, and launch pads, silver and bone-white against the sunburnt earth. It was like a city from the future had crash-landed and decided to stay. Solar arrays gleamed in rigid rows. Pneumatic cranes shifted equipment with the grace of ballet dancers.

Everything was motion and silence and the scent of hot ozone.

"This is it?" Aries asked, breathless. "This is where they train for Mars?"

Commander Noah Karalis gave the faintest smile. "This is where we train."

Aries's eyes flared. That single word, *we*, struck something electric in his chest. He launched forward, his small frame practically vibrating as he sprinted toward the nearest airlock, a light pack bouncing on his back.

Noah watched him go, small and wiry, too young for the weight of his ambitions but already outrunning expectations.

At eleven, Aries sat cross-legged in the AI diagnostics lab, fingers flying across the interface console while code streamed down the curved display. Behind him, three adult engineers watched in mild disbelief.

"He shouldn't even *understand* this interface," one whispered. "It's Tier 4."

"He doesn't just understand it," another muttered. "He's refactoring it."

Lines of messy subroutines disappeared as Aries rewrote an entire logic tree in under ten minutes, stabilizing the comms latency loop that had been causing dropouts across four dome networks. His eyes narrowed in concentration, tongue poking from the corner of his mouth as he isolated an unbalanced recursive call.

"There," he murmured. "The process crashes on the sixth loop. Not from bandwidth, but from a misconfigured base directive overriding the thread handler. It needed a proper lock around the shared resource. That's fixed now."

He leaned back, swiping the diagnostic overlay onto a confirmation screen. The data turned green. Stable.

A silence followed.

"What's his IQ again?" one of the engineers finally asked.

"One-sixty," came the answer. "Officially. Probably higher."

On the observation deck above, Noah said nothing, but his hands relaxed slightly behind his back.

At twelve, Aries was a fixture in the training complex. He jogged laps around the Martian-gravity treadmill, his long limbs growing lean with muscle, his breath steady. Trainers barked instructions, environmental drills, decompression scenarios, rapid evac. Aries responded with a nod or a clipped "copy," his voice already carrying the quiet command of someone older.

After the drills, he didn't rest.

While the others collapsed onto benches or gulped electrolyte packets, Aries pulled up holograms of the habitat blueprints. He cross-referenced air filtration schematics with internal temperature variance reports. One night, an instructor caught him hand-sketching a redesign for the CO_2 scrubber filters using scavenged algae strains from a disused bio-lab proposal.

"You know this was flagged as impractical," she said, arms crossed.

Aries didn't look up. "That was before we discovered the hybrid strain survives in simulated regolith. The resistance values are different now."

The instructor blinked.

"You're twelve," she said.

"I'm twelve and a half," Aries replied, flipping to the next page.

At lights-out, while the dorms dimmed and silence fell, Aries reprogrammed his bunk light to simulate a Martian dawn. He calculated the sun's angle at Eos Chasma to within 0.1 degrees. He did it by hand.

Later that month, during an emergency simulation, Aries was placed solo in a pressurization pod.

"Oxygen fail. Comm loop unstable. Initiating reboot in five…"

Alarms screamed in his ears. Red lights pulsed. The temperature dropped five degrees in thirty seconds.

He didn't panic.

Instead, he traced the fault, by feel, through a tangled power relay schematic that was running a subroutine one layer too deep. He hard-wired a bypass using only the tools in the emergency kit: a strip of polymer, a flex-screw, and his shoelace.

The sequence was completed with two seconds to spare.

His instructor gave a long, low whistle. "Kid's got nerves of steel."

On the other side of the glass, Noah didn't speak. But his eyes followed every movement. Every breath. Every impossible solution.

One evening, Aries joined his father for a maintenance check at the outer dome. It was a quiet task, routine even. But Aries couldn't stop asking questions.

"Why do the polymer seals expand unevenly in vacuum tests?"

"Why use lithium-hydrogel instead of memory foam in the crash couches?"

"What would happen if the hydraulic stabilizers on the rover failed while climbing a slope with a ten-degree yaw?"

Noah answered what he could. For what he couldn't, Aries pulled up schematics and cross-compared designs until he understood.

Understanding wasn't optional. It was his oxygen. His gravity.

He didn't want to just *go* to Mars.

He wanted to *earn* it.

He wanted to know the systems better than the people who built them. To prove every second that he belonged.

Not as a child. Not as a passenger.

But as a Karalis.

As his mother's son.

As the future of a dream that had cost them everything.

ARIES SLOUCHED in his flight jumpsuit, chin propped on one fist, eyes half-lidded as the EVA suit instructor droned on about pressure equalization protocols. Again.

On the screen, a grainy simulation cycled through the steps in monochrome detail — yellow suit indicators, green suit indicators, helmet seals. The same sequence. The same wording. The same tired, over-rehearsed cadence.

Aries had seen this demo six times already.

He'd memorized the pressure thresholds, recalculated the emergency thresholds on his own, and even submitted a revised valve timing protocol that shaved six seconds off depressurization. No one had responded to the report.

So instead of watching, he tapped idly at his tablet, sketching a crude but uncannily accurate caricature of the instructor's shiny bald spot reflecting the simulation lighting.

"Aries," the trainer snapped, not even looking up from the display. "You want to share with the class?"

Aries didn't lift his head. "Only if they're dying to hear how this entire presentation is in the database, verbatim. With worse animations. And somehow less charisma."

A few cadets stifled their laughter.

The instructor exhaled slowly, resisting the urge to respond. "Dismissed."

Aries stood and walked out without waiting for the others.

. . .

COMMANDER KARALIS WAS WAITING in the hallway.

He stood with his arms crossed, boots planted like anchors on the corridor's polished floor. His uniform was pristine as always, face unreadable. The resemblance between them was sharper lately, same jawline, same storm-gray eyes, but there was distance in the space between them, like they belonged to two different atmospheres.

"You skipped pressure tolerance drills again," Noah said.

"They're pointless," Aries replied, not breaking stride. "I've passed the simulation three times. Once with the fail-safe disabled. Once blindfolded, just for fun."

Noah stepped in front of him, blocking his path. "This isn't about passing. It's about discipline. Repetition. You think things won't go wrong out there? That systems won't fail in ways we've never simulated?"

Aries's eyes narrowed. "I think if things go wrong, I'll be the one fixing them while the others panic and read the manual. Again."

"Aries..."

"No," he snapped, louder than he meant to. "You want obedience. You want a little Martian automaton you can plug into your perfect red planet. News flash, I'm not your obedient little soldier."

Noah's jaw tightened. His voice dropped, low and quiet. "You're not a soldier. You're my *son*. And when we land, we'll be relying on each other every hour, every day. That means trust. That means showing up."

Aries stared at him. And for a split second, beneath the defiance, something cracked.

"I was there when she died," he said suddenly, voice like broken glass. "I looked out the window for hours. You were in the dome, running survival drills. You didn't even know she was gone until they called you."

Noah's mouth opened, but no words came.

Aries shook his head. "You weren't there for her. And now you want me to play perfect for you? To pretend this whole colony thing matters more than the fact that she's dead and we're leaving everything behind?"

The silence between them stretched tight, like something that might snap. Aries took a breath, but it trembled.

"Maybe I should just stay on Earth," he muttered, brushing past his father, shouldering him slightly as he walked away. "Maybe you should stay, too."

Noah didn't stop him this time.

He stood in the corridor as the boy he was trying to protect, the boy he was trying to save, walked away carrying more weight than any twelve-year-old should ever bear.

"He's a liability, Karalis," Commander Roland Veyra said as he walked by.

"He is my son," Noah said.

"Talent is only an asset if you can control it," the Wave Two commander remarked. "I wouldn't want him on my team.

And for the first time since the accident, Noah Karalis wasn't sure which of them would survive Mars.

THE LIGHTS WERE out in Dorm Bay 3, but Aries's bunk glowed faintly with the amber warmth of a custom sunrise script he'd rewritten last month. He lay on his side beneath the blanket, tablet cradled to his chest, earbud in place, eyes glassy and unfocused.

"Mom," he whispered.

The screen flickered to life, not with her face exactly, but something like it. A soft-voiced, semi-holographic AI overlay he'd built from thousands of old videos, family logs, facial scans, and snippets of her laugh, her voice, the way she used to say his name when he'd skinned his knee or aced a science fair.

Her image shimmered gently in the air above the tablet, a ghost made of data and memory.

"Hi, baby," she said. That voice. Smooth as wind chimes. "Can't sleep?"

"No," he muttered. "Too much on my mind."

The AI tilted its head. "Want to talk?"

Aries swallowed. He hated how much he needed this. Hated how it helped.

"I keep seeing the door," he said quietly. "You walking out into the storm. I didn't even say thank you. I just lay there like a lump, hacking my lungs out while you…"

He paused, voice catching. The AI was quiet, waiting.

"It should've been nothing. Just cough syrup." His hand curled into the blanket. "If I hadn't been sick, you wouldn't have gone. You'd still be here."

Her voice was gentle, programmed to comfort

but echoing something *real.* "Sweetheart, you didn't make me go. I'm your mom. I wanted to help you."

"But Dad wasn't there," Aries spat, bitterness spilling out. "He was in the damn dome. Oxygen collapse drills. Saving the future. Not *you.* Not us."

The AI said nothing about that. Maybe even it knew better.

"I don't even know if I *want* to go to Mars anymore. What if something goes wrong, and it's like before? What if I screw up again and someone else pays for it?"

The blanket bunched in his fist. "I'm not who he wants me to be. I don't know if I ever was."

Silence.

Then: *"Aries, you're not meant to be someone else. You're meant to be you."*

It wasn't a real answer. But it still felt like her.

He wiped his eyes with the back of his hand, blinking hard at the hologram. "Stupid code," he muttered.

Behind him, something beeped, metal-on-metal, soft and quick. Aries jolted upright.

"What..."

A girl stood in the hatchway, half-shadowed, holding a diagnostic wrench. She froze as soon as he turned.

"Oh, uh, sorry," she stammered. "Didn't know anyone was here. Maintenance request flagged from your dorm pod. The overhead screen is glitching again. I didn't mean to... I thought this unit was empty."

Her voice was light, uncertain, and now that he got a better look, she was definitely his age. Slender black coveralls streaked with wiring dust. Auburn hair pulled into a messy braid. A soldering holster clipped to her belt. Big eyes that had clearly seen way more than their age should allow.

"Hi, I'm Skye Enyo, maintenance cadet. Hope I'm not disturbing you. "

Aries blinked. "No, it's okay, I'm just skipping class. I'm..."

"You're Aries Karalis," she said, stepping forward cautiously. "The boy genius with a trail of broken lighting panels and servos that have been tampered with left behind him. Oh yeah, and the one who reprogrammed the mess hall droid to play grunge during breakfast."

He groaned and flopped back onto the bed. "That was one time. And grunge is an underappreciated music genre. "

She smiled as she began her repair. Then her eyes flicked to the tablet of the AI, his mom's likeness still frozen mid-expression. Her smile faded, realizing she had interrupted a personal moment.

Aries quickly shut it down. "Look, I didn't mean for anyone to..."

Skye held up a hand. "It's okay. I get it."

He studied her face...

Skye closed up the panel she was working on; she was being sincere. "My dad's on Europa Relay Station, been there since I was eight. I built a chatbot interface so I could pretend we were still close. It helped. Sometimes it didn't."

Aries stared at her. For the first time in weeks, someone seemed to understand.

He was not just a prodigy, the program asset, or the Commander's son. He was just a kid who missed his mom.

Skye looked down, almost shy now. "I've been training for 3 years. I'm slotted for Wave Three. If I don't blow up the habitat climate unit next time I run maintenance."

"You won't," Aries said a little too fast. Then quieter: "You're really good. I've seen your repairs."

Her smile returned, this time gentler. "Thanks, I've been watching you too; it's nice having someone to relate to."

An awkward pause stretched between them.

"You know," she said, glancing at the now-dark tablet, "if you ever want to talk. Just break something new for me to fix, and I'll see you."

Aries gave a soft, uncertain laugh. "I might take you up on that; us self-taught kid geniuses need to stick together."

She nodded and then turned to leave but paused at the door.

"We may not be who they want us to be," she said, echoing his own words. "But maybe... We are enough as we are."

Then she was gone, leaving behind the faint scent of solder and something vaguely like cinnamon.

Aries lay back on his bunk, staring at his reflection in the dark screen.

Maybe Mars wouldn't be so lonely after all.

When he got up to leave his quarters, his dad was coming down the hall.

"You missed drills," he said.

"I know I'm sorry. But I did make a friend," Aries replied.

"Aries, this isn't a game. Once we're up there..."

"I know," Aries rolls his eyes. "Once we're up

there, everything changes. No second chances. You've only told me a hundred times."

His dad folded his arms. "So why are you acting like a child?"

"Because I am. I am literally a child!"

The room went silent.

Aries stood his ground, breathing hard. "You keep treating this like it's your big legacy. Your dream. But I didn't get a choice. I didn't get a say. I wasn't asked if I wanted to leave everything behind — our home, Mom's memory...."

And there it was. It seemed like neither of them had fully processed her loss. His dad looked at him then, not as a commander, not as a mission lead, but as a father. One who'd lost his wife. One who didn't know how to talk to the son who'd survived.

"I didn't want to leave you behind," he said quietly.

Aries hesitated. "You could've stayed."

"I couldn't." his dad said. "Not after what happened to your mom. I had to make it mean something."

Aries noticed the truth beneath everything. They were both still grieving. Just doing it at different speeds.

Aries looked away. "I can understand that."

They didn't say goodnight. They didn't need to.

In forty-eight hours, they'd be leaving Earth forever.

Aries looked out his porthole window, memorizing the stars. Wondering which one Mars was passing as it moved in its orbit.

THAT NIGHT, lying in bed, a message popped up on his screen.

"Are you awake?"

He replied, "Who's this?"

"Your favorite fixer."

"Skye?" He typed.

"Yep, I can't sleep. Want to talk?"

They messaged, several hours, learning more about each other, until they both fell asleep.

ARIES WOKE BEFORE HIS ALARM, eyes open to the dark. The old chaos in his head was filled with guilt, anger, and the ache he never outran. Still there. Fine. He set it on a mental shelf. Today he would make it small by outworking it. By out thinking it.

He slid from his bunk, turned off the custom dawn script, and dressed fast.

By the time the dome lights rose, he was already in Bay 2, palms flat on the cold edge of the EVA bench, helmet tucked under one arm. Commander Karalis stood across the room with the lead trainers, surprised, but pleased, when he saw his son in position early.

Morning drills hit like a launch countdown — compressed, precise, and unforgiving.

"Stations in sequence," the instructor called. "Pressure, comms, nav, life-support triage, rover ascent. No external prompts. You know the rules."

STATION 1: Pressure

Aries didn't answer. He sealed his helmet.

A soft hiss. The world narrowed to breath and numbers.

He ran the suit checks without looking at the prompts. Touch-memory, crisp and exact. Seal integrity, green. Differential equalization, smooth. He preempted a known micro-spike by feathering the valve 0.4 seconds early, flattening the curve before the system flagged it. Time-to-ready: 00:42, a full eleven seconds under spec.

"Mark," someone said, almost under their breath.

· · ·

STATION 2: Comms

Latency injection started at 220 milliseconds; he felt it more than saw it. He re-coded the buffer priorities on the fly, siphoning bandwidth from idle telemetry to voice with a two-line hot patch. Ping fell to 78ms. He toggled to back up and back again, checking for echo. Clean.

"Who taught him that bypass?" an engineer whispered.

"He teaches himself," Skye's voice replied from the mezzanine.

Station 3: Navigation

The sim threw him into a low-visibility dust challenge, false slope cues, yaw drift, stale light detection and ranging sensor returns. Aries ignored the noisy feed and trusted the inertial measurement unit signature, cross-checking against wheel slip and motor draw. He cut speed, corrected yaw by three degrees, faced the slope, and crested without a single traction error.

Station 4: Life-Support Triage

A cascade failure test — subtle, nasty. He didn't chase the alarm; he hunted for the cause. With CO_2 rising, O_2 stable. That meant scrubbers, not leaks.

He tore the panel, swapped the cartridge, rerouted flow around a sticky valve with a glove gasket and two clamps. Levels normalized in forty-one seconds. The trainer looked down at the stopwatch as if it had lied to him. Aries just grinned. He knew his abilities, and they did too now.

STATION 5: Rover Ascent

Final run. He threaded the rover up the simulated basalt steps, never once slamming the dampers. Gas, brake, glide. He treated the machine like an animal that wanted to live.

The bay fell silent as he rolled to a perfect stop.

"Time," the instructor called. He sounded offended at his own awe. "Seventeen minutes, twelve seconds. New course record."

A murmur ran through the room. Not all of it was friendly. A few first-wave candidates looked away, cheeks tight. One shook his head, muttering something about "showboating."

Skye didn't care. She whooped from the rail, both hands over her head, braid whipping her shoulder. "Let's go, Karalis!"

Aries popped his helmet, breath fogging in the cool air. He didn't smile, not exactly, but the set of his jaw softened. He looked up and found Skye. She flashed a thumbs-up, then a small, private nod that said: *I see you. Keep going.*

"Run him again," one trainer said.

"Different order," another added. "Stack the failures."

They did. Three more full-circuit drills, each harder than the last, unexpected decompression, sensor lies, a dead servo mid-climb. Aries treated each like a puzzle he'd already solved in a dream. He never rushed; he just refused to waste motion.

When he finished, sweat pasted his hair to his forehead, and his under-suit clung to his spine. His metrics were obscene: fastest composite time, lowest error count, best oxygen management.

"Aries," the instructor said finally, voice neutral to try to hide what it couldn't. "Dismissed."

He stepped back from the rover, unsnapping his gloves, and almost ran into Commander Karalis. Noah's eyes held pride and something rougher — relief, maybe, or fear disguised as gratitude.

"Good work," his father said quietly.

Aries nodded once. "Copy."

It wasn't forgiveness. Not yet. But it wasn't nothing.

As the bay emptied, a cluster of first-wave crew

lingered, their conversations low and tight. A few glares slid off Aries like dust. Shame wasn't his to carry today.

Skye trotted down the stairs to meet him, tablet tucked to her chest, cheeks still flushed. "You were ridiculous," she said. "In a good way. Like, offensively competent."

"Offensively?" he echoed, deadpan.

"Yeah. You hurt their feelings with your excellence." She leaned in, grin crooked. "Also, that comms hotpatch? I'm stealing it to fix Bay 4. Your method could stabilize the drone relay through the north wall."

"Use it," he said. "It's cleaner if you open the mutex lock."

"I knew you were going to say that." She slapped his shoulder. "Come on. Hydrate before someone decides you're a machine and forgets you're still human."

As they walked, a tech called after them, half-joking, half-resentful, "Hey, Karalis, you killed it, thanks for making us all look bad."

Skye didn't slow, but her voice went level. "He's not jealous or anything. He'll be glad you are with them when the planet tries to kill you."

Silence behind them. The kind that sounded a lot like acceptance.

They hit the water station. Aries drank, throat working, breath steadying, the burn in his muscles settling into something almost like calm. Skye leaned beside him, shoulder-to-shoulder, close but not crowding.

"Wave Three feels a little closer today," she said softly.

He glanced at her. "Today felt... less far."

She studied his face. "You okay?"

He thought of the shelf in his head, the box with the ache inside it. He thought of his father's quiet good work. Of the way the bay had gone still when everything he could do silenced everything he couldn't say.

"I will be," he said.

Skye nodded, as if that was the right answer, even if it wasn't the final one. "Good. Because tomorrow I'm timing you. And I heckle."

"You heckle?"

"Professionally."

His mouth twitched. "Copy."

They moved back toward the floor, where the bay lights hummed and the world smelled like ozone and rubber. Aries pulled his helmet on again, weight settling familiar and solid in his hands.

Do it right. Do it clean. Do it again.

Aries like this new tactic of rebellion; show them what they can't do.

If he couldn't fix the past, he would build a future that didn't break. And for the first time since the storm, he believed he could.

4

T-MARK 24 HOURS

The countdown crawled across every monitor, a silent metronome in red numerals: T–24:00:00.

Aries Karalis stood in the doorway of Dorm Bay 3 with his duffel on the floor and the life he wasn't taking laid out on the bed. The room was quieter than usual. His bunk light, still running his custom Martian dawn script, glowed a soft amber, bleeding over the edges of a folded sweatshirt, a paper book of Greek myths and a model of the first model rocket he and his mom had built together. He traced the rocket's tiny fins with a thumb. The glue blob along the edge was his impatient mistake. Mom had laughed and called it "Aries' signature."

He put the model in the "taking" pile.

He wasn't taking much. There wasn't room for much.

The standard kit took most of the duffel: thermal layers, med patch strips, a compact toolkit he'd customized with a few contraband bits (a micro torque driver, a loop of wire, a line-cutter meant for EVA but just as good for wild cabling), two data wafers he'd crammed with books and music and a folder labeled Mom. He couldn't leave the AI; he needed her; he needed to be able to talk to her.

A chime announced someone at the hatch.

"Open," he called to the automated door.

Skye Enyo slid in sideways, as if unsure of her welcome. She wore dark coveralls smeared with conduit dust, braid lopsided like she'd rebuilt a turbine and then sprinted here. A small kit bag hit her hip with a solid thunk as she closed the door behind her with one boot.

"Karalis," she said, then immediately softened. "Hey."

"Oh, hey." He half-smiled. "Got any advice on packing? This sentimental Tetris is making my head hurt."

She tilted her head at the bed. "Is that the bear, the one your mother left you with that night?"

He nodded.

"Take it," she said, no hesitation. "You need something meaningful and important to look at when a regulator alarm won't shut up."

He put it inside a mesh pouch and tucked it between thermal socks.

Skye hovered, reached out, stopped. "I brought you something." She dug in her kit and pulled a small square wrapped in foil. "Don't make a face."

"What is it?"

"Cinnamon gum." She shrugged. "My mom's superstition. Before every major inspection, I chew a piece. It was my mother's 'test-day thing.' You can't bring sticks of luck on the manifest, so I disguised it as thermal tape."

He laughed. "You smuggled gum?"

"Say you're grateful before I change my mind."

"I'm grateful." He took the square, peeled back the foil, and held it up like a relic. "I'll use it when it matters."

"Like the first time the habitat toilet screams at two in the morning." She perched on the edge of his bunk, studying his face. "You look... okay."

"Define okay."

"Like someone holding a heavy thing correctly." She glanced at the countdown on the wall. T–23:14:12. "Have you seen your dad yet?"

"After I finish here," he said. "Ready room briefing at eighteen hundred. Graveyard at sixteen." He heard how that sounded. "I didn't mean it like that. I need to say goodbye."

"It's okay; we deal with loss in our own way, no judgment." She nudged the duffel with a toe. "You want help folding? I'm pretty good at creases?"

"I can manage my own creases," he said. He squared a shirt just to prove it.

Silence settled between them, not awkward, just dense. The weight of the next day pressed in from all directions, metal and schedule and the knowledge that some doors only opened once.

Skye looked at his hands. "Can I ask you something that's not in any training manual?"

He nodded.

"Are you scared?"

He thought about it honestly. "Yes," he said. "Not of the launch. Of failing at the thing that matters. Of messing up the part that's not fixable with a patch or a wire."

"People," she said.

"People," he echoed. "My dad. You. The crew. Me."

"You don't owe anyone a perfect version of yourself," she said. "Just the honest one."

He almost made a joke about honesty being inefficient in a crisis but didn't. He slid the gum into his breast pocket instead, a tiny square of Earth disguised as tape.

She stood and then lingered. The air smelled faintly of solder and cinnamon. "I'll see you before the ready room," she said.

"Skye..." he started and failed to line up the words.

She saved him. "I'm rooting for you," she said simply. "And not just because your comms patches make my job easier."

He swallowed. "Copy."

She smiled and slipped out. The hatch clicked shut. The quiet returned.

He zipped the duffel, slung it over his shoulder, and took one last look at the room. The dawn script painted the wall a soft, rising orange. He reached up and killed it. Night fell in a heartbeat.

T–22:50:08

Commander Noah Karalis's office felt like a place evacuated of air. The windows looked out over Launch Complex Theta, a bone-white set of towers and gantries etched black by shadows. The copper wash of late afternoon hit the glass at an angle that flared the dust hanging in the air.

Noah wasn't behind his desk. He was standing by the window with his back turned, hands clasped behind him in a posture that said he'd been standing there a long time. The uniform was clean, sharp even. The man inside it looked like someone who had forgotten how to sleep.

Aries closed the door behind him. "You wanted to see me."

His dad turned. For a heartbeat, something almost soft flickered across his face at seeing his son standing there with his duffel — pride, fear, love, some impossible mix of them all. Then the command mask settled. He gestured to the two chairs in front of the desk.

"Sit," Noah said. "You're ten minutes early."

"I'm tired of being late to conversations that are important," Aries said, and sat.

They didn't speak for a moment. The countdown marched on, silent and palpable: T–22:49:17.

"I read your drills," Noah said finally. "All of them. Today. Yesterday. The week before."

"Numbers are friendly," Aries said.

"You were more than numbers," Noah said, allowing the smallest of smiles. "You were calm. Precise. You showed restraint."

"Trying a new thing."

"Keep it," Noah said. He leaned forward, elbows to knees. "We need to talk about the next twenty-four hours like we won't get another chance."

Aries nodded, pulse tapping at his throat.

"First," Noah said, voice even, "I'm proud of you. Not just for the records you broke; for showing up when it would be easier to run. I know what you're carrying. I don't expect it to weigh less just because we cross an atmosphere."

Aries stared at his hands. "I was cruel," he said. "In the hall."

"You were honest," Noah said softly. "And I earned some of that."

A fault line cracked open in Aries's chest. "She went out because of me; it's my fault."

"She went out because she loved you," Noah said. "I know that doesn't make the ache less. But I hope it changes how you carry the guilt. She would forgive you in an instant if she could."

Aries's throat tightened. "I don't want to hate you," he said, voice small and fierce. "I don't want to go with you to Mars and build a life out of resentment."

"I don't want that either," Noah said. He shifted closer, not touching, just there. "So let's make a deal. We build a place where grief is allowed to sit at the table, but it doesn't get to captain the ship. We keep each other honest and alive. We ask for help before the air runs out."

Aries breathed out, shaky. "Copy."

Noah's eyes shone, just for a second. He glanced out the window. "You're going to the cemetery?"

Aries nodded.

"I'll give you the time," Noah said. He stood and then hesitated. "One more thing."

Aries looked up.

Noah reached into his desk and pulled out a small, flat box. Inside, on a strip of fabric, rested his mission patch, Noah's, stitched with a narrow strand of red thread along the edge.

"Your mother did that," Noah said, almost smiling. "Said my patch needed luck that didn't look like luck so the engineers wouldn't confiscate it."

Aries laughed once. "Skye brought me gum disguised as thermal tape."

"She's resourceful," Noah said, with a note of something curious in his voice. "Take this." He lifted the patch and pressed it into Aries's hands. "Sew it inside your collar. Don't let regulation see it."

"Is that an order?"

"That's a father asking his son to carry something small and stubborn to a place far away."

Aries slid the patch into his pocket, a second contraband talisman.

"See you at eighteen hundred," Noah said.

Aries stood, and for a second they didn't know how to part. Then Noah reached for him, and Aries stepped into the space, and the hug was awkward only in the way that both of them were trying not to break.

When Aries left the office, the dust in the hall looked like snow.

T–21:15:40

The cemetery was tucked into a sloped piece of ground beyond the training domes, where the desert wore its age openly and the wind kept secrets. Solar glass markers caught the light, each a quiet panel that could display a name, a date, a message, a photograph that only the registered could see.

Aries walked the path he'd memorized, past the low wall and the single scrub tree that insisted on being alive. He stopped at Eleni Karalis. The panel lit as he approached, a soft glow rising like someone waking.

He knelt. For a long time, he did nothing at all.

"Hi, Mom," he said finally, voice rough. The wind carried the smell of dust and heat. "I don't know what to say that I haven't already said into a screen with your voice coming out of it."

The panel warmed under his fingers. A photo she'd loved flickered up, her hand on a rocket model, laughing at the camera because Aries had knocked over a bottle of paint. He'd been seven. He could still hear the laugh. Less sharp now, but it was there.

"I'm going," he said. "You knew I would. You probably knew before I did."

His mouth twisted. "I'm scared that if I get good at living somewhere else, I'll forget what it meant to live here with you. I'm scared I'll fix everything that can be fixed and still fail at the part where a person needs me and I'm in the wrong room."

The wind hissed softly across the panels. Someone far away laughed, then quieted.

"I was angry at Dad," he admitted. "I still am sometimes. It's just... less messy today. I think he's scared too. That helps." He swallowed. "I want to do this right. Not perfect. Right."

He reached into his breast pocket and took out the foil square. He peeled it open and set the stick of gum at the base of the panel. "Skye says luck tastes like cinnamon."

He took the mission patch from his other pocket,

too, his mother's red stitch winking in the low light. He pressed it against the glass. "I'll wear this where no one can see it," he whispered. "Except maybe you."

For a while he just breathed with the desert, slow and even, and let the anger and the ache and the love sit beside him like companions that didn't always talk.

When he stood, the sun had tilted. He touched the name one last time.

"See you on the other side of the solar system," he said. "I miss you every day."

He walked back toward the complex, lighter and heavier in equal measure.

T–18:03:12

The ready room looked like every movie about space had tried to copy it and failed. Thirty seats in three arcs, screens wrapping the walls, a central table with the mission crest—and bowls of pale protein cubes that no one ever ate unless a briefing ran long.

The Wave One crew filled the room with nervous competence. Jumpsuits zipped; hair braided tight; voices pitched low. A few of the older hands were unembarrassed enough to be excited. Most just looked like people doing a job they'd trained their entire lives to do while trying not to think about the part where the job could kill them.

Aries slipped in and took a seat along the second arc. A couple of side glances slid his way; a few nods, terse but real. He noted who sat with whom, who fidgeted, who drank water, who pretended not to notice the countdown might as well be tattooed on everyone's eyelids.

Skye wasn't there, Wave Three had their own room and a haze of envy and dread. But as he adjusted his collar, his finger found the mission patch sewn inside, hidden stitch by hidden stitch, the red thread rough like a heartbeat. He pictured her rolling her eyes at the protein cubes. He smiled without meaning to.

The door at the front hissed open. Director Erick Caulder walked in first, steel gray suit, hair clipped razor neat, a man who lived inside constraints and wielded them like tools. Behind him came Commander Karalis, suit black and severe, expression spare, eyes sweeping the room for threats that weren't here yet.

A third figure entered and took a place by the systems wall, Dr. Sierra, mission psych, tablet under one arm like a truth detector.

Caulder didn't waste time. "Wave One," he said,

voice carrying easily without amplification. "Thank you for being on time."

A ripple of dry amusement. He had that effect, demanding and somehow human.

"This will be the last briefing before you enter prep quarantine," he continued. "You know the manifest. You know the risks. You know your roles. Today is about clarity and cadence."

He gestured to the wall display. Seven silhouettes resolved into portraits, then into names and departments. "For those of you who haven't had the pleasure of being yelled at by all of them, meet your Systems Officers, the seven people who will keep you alive when the planet and the hardware conspire in chaos."

Aries leaned forward, alert, pencil poised though he could have written the bios from memory. He liked seeing how they introduced themselves more than the words on their personnel files.

"Dr. Evelyn Moreau, Systems Officer: Life Support." A woman in her late forties with close-cropped hair and a sleeve of faded tattoos peeking from under her cuff raised a hand. "If it moves air, water, or heat, it's mine," she said, her Texas drawl buried under years of careful speech. "If you breathe wrong near my scrubbers, I'll know."

"Lieutenant James Rogers, Systems Officer: Navigation and Guidance." Sleek, thin, with a pilot's shoulders and a mathematician's eyes. "I am the reason we don't drift into a very bad day," he said. "If you feel lost, you are. Ask me anyway."

"Dr. Yara Valli, Systems Officer: Structures and Habitat." Tall, blunt, hands like a sculptor. "I designed half the bones of the place you'll call home," she said. "Don't test the other half."

"Chief Roger Bennett, Systems Officer: Power and Thermal." Mid-thirties, restless energy, grease still in the lines of his palm. "If it makes electricity, heat, or a fuss, I speak its language," he said. "If I tell you to turn something off, don't ask why—count how long you've been alive and add to it."

"Dr. Sophia Adamos, Systems Officer: Biology and External Environments." A biologist with patient eyes and boots that had seen field mud. "I will keep your insides from becoming your outsides," she said. "Also, don't lick Mars."

Laughter broke the tension. She didn't smile.

"Chief Petty Officer Danika Vost, Systems Officer: EVA and Mobility." Stocky, a scar across one eyebrow, a presence that made you check your posture. "I care about your suits, your rovers, and whether you think you're invincible," she said. "Two of those are fixable."

"And finally," Caulder said, with a glance that almost, almost softened, "Dr. Nate Reese, Systems Officer: Communications and Network." A man — perhaps unfairly young to be the architect of so much infrastructure — sharp, quiet, the kind of person who wrote code you could trust in a storm. "If your voice goes somewhere," he said, "I shepherded it. If it doesn't, I'm already building you a better path."

Aries felt a flicker of pleasure that someone else spoke about comms like that—with reverence, not just utility.

Caulder clasped his hands. "These seven will triage in a cascade event. Listen to them. If they disagree, Commander Karalis decides."

Thirty heads turned to Noah. He stood a beat longer than necessary, letting the weight of authority settle where it belonged.

"We have practiced failing," he said, voice clean and unadorned. "We will practice succeeding. Between those poles sits the work. You know the checklists. You know your partner's tells. You know the anchor points on your harness without looking."

He let the room breathe.

"And still, something will surprise us," he said. "When it does, we slow down, we tell the truth, and we do the next correct thing."

Aries wrote that without realizing it, the next correct thing, as if it were a new law of physics.

Caulder stepped back in. "Two items. First: manifest addendum is final. No changes. Second, psychological readiness is not a checkbox. If you need to talk, do it. Dr. Sierra will be in the quarantine bay, and confidentiality holds."

Dr. Sierra nodded once. "You do not have to hurt alone," she said, and somehow made it sound like instructions instead of comfort.

Questions followed, ration matrices, burn windows, dust probability at the secondary landing. Rogers and Bennett argued amicably about load shedding. Vost warned about an oddity in the left hip ring of the new generation suit. Reese outlined a plan to piggyback status bursts on low-bandwidth telemetry if the relay stuttered.

Aries asked one question about buffer allocation priorities during simultaneous EVA feeds and environmental alarms. Wagner's eyes lit. "Exactly," he said. "We'll use your hotpatch with a mutex variation. Are you free to test after the briefing?"

Aries glanced at Noah, who kept his face still but

his nod was small and sure. "Yes," Aries said. "I'm free."

"Good," Reese said. "Bring the gum," he added dryly, glancing at the cinnamon-sweet scent in the air that Skye had somehow smuggled through the walls of memory. Aries blinked, then realized the officer was joking. The room slipped another thin ripple of laughter that made everything feel less brittle.

Caulder watched the exchange and then consulted the clock. T–17:11:29. "That's it. Quarantine begins at nineteen hundred. Loved ones, now or never," he said, uncharacteristically gentle. "No grand speeches. Just do your jobs."

Chairs scraped. People stood. The ready room emptied in a tide.

Noah approached Aries, and for a moment they simply existed side by side, two points in a line that ran from a rainy night to a red planet.

"Systems bay in twenty?" Noah said.

"Reese wants to test the patch."

"Then go," Noah said. "I'll meet you after."

Aries turned to leave and almost ran into Caulder. He studied him with an unsparing gaze that didn't feel like judgment so much as inventory.

"Karalis," he said.

"Director."

"You're not your father, which is good."

He felt heat rise to his face, of embarrassment and of relief. "I try to be my best."

"Also good," he said. A pause. "And for what it's worth, Eleni would have told me to get out of your way."

The sentence landed like a benediction. Aries nodded, unable to trust his voice. Caulder stepped aside.

T–16:42:50

The corridor outside was less formal, more human. People hugged. People pretended not to. Techs made jokes about oxygen smells. A pilot set an alarm to remind himself to cry later. The ordinary strangeness of leaving everything.

Skye appeared as she always did, in motion. She checked a panel with one hand while tucking a stray lock of hair with the other. Aries found himself watching her more than was necessary. He didn't care that in less than a day he was leaving and might never see her again. He still wanted to see her now while he could. When she saw him, the motion paused.

"How was the speechifying?" she asked.

"Tolerable. Useful. Bennett made a power joke."

"I hate that I missed it."

"You didn't," he said. "He'll tell it again. It's self-replicating."

She snorted. Her gaze flicked to his collar. "You did the thing."

"I did the thing."

"Good," she said, suddenly serious. She stepped closer, eyes on his. A dozen sounds filled the hall — boots, clips, distant laughter — but they fell back from the bubble around them.

"I know you don't need luck," she said softly. "You make your own."

He almost made a quip and didn't. He only nodded.

"But I'm going to be superstitious anyway," she added, voice lighter now. "For me."

Before he could ask what that meant, she rose on her toes and kissed him. It wasn't quick. It wasn't dramatic. It tasted like cinnamon and dust and a small, stubborn future. It hit him like stepping into gravity after a long float — surprising, right, inevitable? He held her, prolonging the kiss. He loved the way it made him feel. Maybe it was her and not just the feeling of it.

When she pulled back, her cheeks were pink.

Her grin tried to be cocky and almost made it. "For luck," she said unnecessarily.

He breathed out, a sound halfway to a laugh. "I'll see you soon."

"I hope so," she said. "Because I'm not building Wave Three's hydro loop without the person who made the comms stop stuttering."

He wanted to say a thousand things, about how scared he was, about how much he liked that she'd found him under all the armor, about how he wanted to see what her braid did in Mars light, but he felt the systems bay pulling at him and the clock chasing them both.

"See you on the other side of the solar system," he said.

She nodded, eyes bright. "Go; I'll be there soon enough. "

T–12:00:00 to T–00:30:00

The last twelve hours blurred into a single, tireless line: patch tests with Reese (the mutex variation held under false alarm flood, and Aries felt the strange calm of watching something he'd made carry weight); a final suit fit with Vost, "You grow one millimeter on the ride and I'll know". Aries ran a scrubber check with Moreau, where she pretended not to be impressed; he did a habitat door sim with Valli that made him swear he would never underestimate a hinge again.

Bennett fed him an electrolyte packet that tasted like submissive lemons and asked about his favorite algorithm, which felt like affection. Rogers let him drive a rover sim along a ridgeline, and he only flinched once. Adamos warned him about Martian dust and irritations until he promised to be careful.

In the quarantine bay, Dr. Sierra asked if he wanted to talk. He said, "Maybe later," and eventually he did. He said the words guilt and anger and love out loud to someone with a quiet face, and it didn't make him weaker.

He slept in ninety-minute slices, waking each time convinced there was something else to fix. There wasn't. He made a list anyway.

T–00:20:00

They walked to the gantry in two lines, suits half-sealed, helmets cradled like eggs. The desert had pulled its old trick of pretending to be gentle. The sky was a color that didn't have a name.

Aries fell into step beside Noah. Neither spoke for a while.

"You ready?" Noah said at last.

"No," Aries said. "But I'm right."

Noah smiled, the kind that reached his eyes. "That will do."

The vehicle waited, white and impossible, asleep and dreaming of flame.

Aries glanced back once. The complex spread behind them, domes and towers and people who'd taught him how to be a person. He thought of Skye in Bay 4, pretending not to look at the clock. He touched his collar at the hidden patch, then his pocket at the empty foil. He felt for the first time that he could hold all of this without dropping it.

At the base of the elevator, the systems officers stood like saints you could actually talk to. Moreau thumped his shoulder. Rogers offered a tiny bow. Valli pointed two fingers at her eyes and then at him: watch your corners. Bennett handed him a real lemon candy and wouldn't take it back. Adamos said, "Breathe." Vost said, "Don't do anything heroic. Do the checklists." Reese just said, "See you on channel."

Aries stepped into the lift beside his father as the doors slid shut. The floor hummed.

The clock hit T–00:19:59.

He didn't feel the old panic. He felt a settling. A baseline.

He pictured a cemetery panel in the late sun, a gum wrapper at its base. He pictured a girl with dust on her cheek and a kiss on her lips saying, *for luck.* He pictured Earth above a conference table turning in a slow, blue spin and didn't feel betrayed by its beauty.

"Next correct thing," he murmured.

"Copy," Noah said, without asking what he meant.

The elevator rose.

5

FAREWELL

T −00:12:00

The gantry elevator delivered them into white light and noise — humming pumps, whispering fans, the impatient throb of a vehicle that wanted to be a star. The stack loomed against the desert sky: three stages in series, capped by the transfer stage and the pressurized crew module like a pearl in a spear point. On its flank, stenciled in sober black: TITAN X - WAVE ONE.

Thirty of them moved in two files, helmets cradled in the crooks of arms, suit umbilicals trailing like leashes to the wall racks. Crew techs in orange vests ghosted around them, tugging zippers, tapping gauges, murmuring checklists.

Aries felt the world narrow to breath, heartbeat,

and the tiny abrasion of the hidden mission patch against his collar, a scratch of red thread no regulation could find.

"Eyes up," Chief Vost said at the hatch, voice a drill bit. "Stick to your seat map. Stow list in your head or not at all."

He knew it through muscle memory. Aries slotted down the tube and into the pressurized crew module, the world shrinking from cathedral to cockpit. He snapped into Seat 9A, forward starboard, just behind the central stack where Commander Karalis settled with the pilot cadre and Systems Officer Rogers. Across the aisle, Life Support's Dr. Moreau tugged her straps into submission; Bennett, Power/Thermal, muttered to himself in a marriage of math and superstition. In the aft ring, Dr. Wagner brought comms online, hands moving with the easy speed of someone who knew where every ghost lived inside the network.

Aries cinched his harness and opened his console. The screen lit up with: cabin vitals, suit vitals, ascent profile, error log (empty), debug backdoor (his), and a muted chat window where someone was already posting *Keep your head up AK*, signed S.E. He smiled and minimized it before he could be tempted to reply.

The hatch sealed with a thump Aries felt through his ribs.

"Flight, Booster, go/no-go." CAPCOM's voice was cool water over the radio.

"Booster is go."

"Flight Dynamics, go/no-go."

"Flight Dynamics go."

"Guidance."

"Guidance go." The cadence settled into a drum-beat. Systems Officers called internal checks in parallel.

"Life Support green," Moreau said.

"Power/Thermal nominal," Bennett added, fingers dancing.

"Structures locked," Valli called, barely glancing up.

"EVA/Mobility secured," Vost grunted.

"Navigation green," Rogers said.

"Biology/Enviro green," Adamos reported.

"Comms online, primary and secondary. Tertiary is listening," Reese added. "No echo."

Commander Karalis's voice entered the loop last. "Wave One is go."

Aries flexed his hands inside the gloves, making small circles to clear the jitter. He'd trained for this climb a hundred times. He knew where the vehicle would creak, where the alarms were loud and harmless, and where they were soft and lethal.

T–00:00:10. The hold-downs armed with a sharp clack.

"Nine—" CAPCOM said, and the world held its breath.

"Eight... seven..."

Aries closed his eyes to a single, stubborn image: a cinnamon kiss and a smile that had tried to play it off.

"Six... five..."

He opened them.

"Four... three..."

"Range is green."

"Two..."

Ignition.

The sound came first, a low rumble, like thunder rolling across the desert. Then the rocket shook so hard it felt like the whole world was trying to tear Aries out of his seat. Force slammed him back, pinning him as the launch pad dropped away. The sky peeled from blue to purple to black.

"Roll program," a voice said. The rocket tilted, and Aries felt the twist in his gut, like a leaf caught in the wind.

"Pitch." The ship angled again. Across his screen,

numbers streamed by. Valli's jaw clenched; her readouts stayed green.

"Booster cutoff. Stage sep nominal." The first stage fell away with a kick he felt in his teeth. Second stage lit, steady as a heart you could calibrate.

Aries breathed when the pilot did. He felt the cabin settle into the long climb.

"Stand by for the third stage..."

A sudden alert from the error log sounded; Aries's eyes flicked right. A yellow flag bloomed, then red: PYRO LINE INHIBIT / UMBILICAL: CONNECTED.

Umbilical... connected? They were ten seconds from separation. There was nothing to be connected to.

"Flight, we have a sensor fault on the third-stage separation interlock," Reese said, voice clipped but even. "Umbilical false positive."

"Confirm," Valli snapped. "I'm seeing inhibit."

"Guidance," Rogers warned, "we need that sensor on the timeline or our burn profile will..."

"... go to garbage," Bennett finished. "Power surge risk if we fire through a stuck inhibit."

Aries didn't wait for permission to open the debug backdoor. He knew the sub-controller, the interstage release logic tree, like a bad dream. He'd lived in it last winter when a sim rig had developed a similar ghost. The problem: a stuck bit in the umbilical sense line told the controller the vehicle was still mated to ground umbilical. Manual override — a guarded toggle — would fire the pyros, anyway. But if the inhibit high fed through the bus at the wrong microsecond, the controller could interpret a short and drop the firing sequence entirely, or worse, trip the main bus protect and kill guidance mid-burn.

"Manual?" Vost barked, hand hovering over the guard. "Say the word."

"Negative," Aries said before he could stop himself. He heard the intake of breath around him. He was thirteen. He was not in the chain of command, but he pressed on, fast and clear. "The inhibit line is stuck high. Manual through a false high risks back feeding into the bus. We'll lose the sequence and trigger the engine cutout."

Reese swore under his breath once. "He's right."

"Flight?" CAPCOM's voice was a tight wire.

"Hold manual," Noah said, calm as a metronome. To Aries: "You have a better way. Say it."

Aries's hands moved. "We cut the false bit at the software level. Bypass the umbilical check, route the firing logic to the clean path, and time the pyro with a three-millisecond delay to avoid the cutoff. The controller never sees the bad line."

"Can you do it fast?" Rogers asked, not unkind.

"Doing it," Aries said. He pulled up the controller's microservice, fingers flying. He inserted a tiny patch, a six-line override that told the release logic to trust the inertial separation timer, not the umbilical sensor, and to hold the bus protect off for a breath's width at the moment of firing.

"Comms, push," Reese said, already opening the pipe. "I'll shepherd."

"Power, can you live with the protect hold?" Bennett asked himself aloud, then nodded. "I can."

"Structures, any objection?" Noah asked.

"I'm not sure," Valli said. "Do it."

"Three seconds to window," Rogers warned.

"Patch loaded," Reese said. "Controller shows green."

Aries hit EXECUTE.

For an instant, nothing happened. The cabin tightened around thirty pairs of lungs.

Then the interstage bolts blew with a percussive CRACK, clean and final. The third stage drifted away like a bad thought. The transfer stage shuddered and then caught, engine lighting with a push that put a new kind of weight in Aries's chest.

"Separation confirmed," CAPCOM said, and something like laughter ran around the room, too sharp with adrenaline to be joy.

Aries let his head tip back against the seat for a count of two and then looked down again. No red. Telemetry stabilized. Guidance nudged them onto the corridor. Bennett murmured a thanks to physics. Reese's hands stilled, then found something else to do out of habit.

Noah's voice came through his headset, not on loop, just seat-to-seat, private. "Nice work."

Aries swallowed. "Copy."

They rode the last burn like a promise to orbit, edges of vision pulsing with the long acceleration. When the engine finally cut, the silence was absolute and huge. Straps hung with new purpose. A pen floated past Aries's cheek, turning lazy cartwheels until someone snared it.

"We are in orbit," CAPCOM said, a little breathless despite themselves. "Welcome, Wave One."

Cheers, real ones this time, broke open and clattered around the module. Someone whooped. Someone else cried without trying to hide it. Aries uncurled his fingers and found crescents in his palms where nails had pressed.

Skye's muted chat window blinked once with a single message that slid through even his filters, a high-priority ping from Wave Three Ops: S.E.: You did it. He didn't answer. He would later. He let himself imagine cinnamon for one second, then let it go.

Rendezvous orbit was work. Orbit was always work. They had forty-one minutes to do a systems-scan, micro-correct, and line up the approach to the Hercules tanker, an ugly, beautiful drum with engines and hoses, a flying gas station that looked like a floating octopus. Rogers's hands were quiet and sure. Vost's mouth moved with throne-room profanity at a stubborn latch that wasn't even hers to fix yet. Bennett watched the power curve like a gambler who knew the house could be kind if you respected it.

"Comms, Lock. A and B telemetry connected," Reese said. "Karalis, watch the buffer window. If Hercules coughs, I want your hotpatch ready."

"On it," Aries said. The patch sat there like a loaded but safe thing. The tanker didn't cough. They docked on the second microburst with a soft kiss and a set of clunks that felt like a door closing and opening at once.

"Fuel transfer nominal," CAPCOM intoned.

"The projected window for Trans-Mars Injection burn opens in forty."

The words hit Aries low and deep. He felt the shape of the flight path in his bones: a long, elliptical highway where you fell in the right direction for half a year and called it flight.

Valli floated by to check a panel, boots magnetizing thunk-thunk to the deck with easy grace. She spared Aries a glance that was almost a smile.

He let himself look out a port for the first time. Earth was a blue eye rimmed in white, too whole to resent. He thought of a cemetery panel, a scrub tree, a gum wrapper; he pressed his tongue to his teeth and tasted the cinnamon still.

"Karalis," Chief Vost said, catching his attention with the hook of her voice as the module settled into the practical monotony that follows terror. She jerked her chin toward the forward bulkhead, where the Systems Officers liked to argue out of the way. "With me."

He followed, feeling eyes on his back, some approving, some calculating, some simply curious about the kid who had reached into the vehicle's heart and told it a new story mid-flight.

Vost crossed her arms. Valli leaned against the bulkhead. Reese hovered nearby, already wary.

Bennett whistled tunelessly to make the space less sharp.

"You saved our asses," Vost said. "And I don't say that lightly. But we need to talk about the way you did it."

Aries kept his face open. "Okay."

"You had a manual override with one motion and one risk. You chose to code a fix during ascent."

"One risk?" Aries repeated, carefully. "Manual through an inhibit high could have tripped main bus protect and..."

"... and it didn't," Vost cut in. "Because we didn't throw it."

"Because it might have," Bennett said gently, interposing. "Manual under a false umbilical read is not the same risk as a clean manual."

Vost's eyes didn't leave Aries. "We have procedures for a reason. When the vehicle is doing sixty-five hundred meters per second and wants to come apart, the person with the least blood sugar and the most adrenaline should not be writing code."

"I agree," Aries said, surprising them and himself. "I wasn't the person with the lowest blood sugar."

Something almost like humor flickered across Vost's scar. "Cute."

Aries took a breath. "I didn't default to the patch because I wanted to be clever. I did it because manual was upstream of a bad bit that would have lied to the controller and maybe cost us the sequence. The software path was the only one that could ignore the lie and still protect power."

"Is there a world," Valli asked, voice calm as stone, "in which you would have thrown manual?"

"Yes," Aries said. "If the bus had sagged, if the controller glitched, if Reese hadn't been there to shepherd the packet, if we were past the window and had to take a dirtier separation. If any of those were true, I'd have hit the guard and thrown the switch myself."

Reese nodded, slow. "He's not wrong, Danika."

Vost blew out through her nose. The heat softened, leaving only steel. "Fine. You made the right call. But hear me, Karalis: sometimes you don't have your pet code or your best day. Sometimes the move is ugly and manual and costs you something you can count. When that day comes, I don't want to see you hesitate because elegance feels better than force."

Aries held her gaze. "Copy."

"Say it like you mean it," she said.

"I hear you," he said, this time letting it land

behind his teeth. "I won't romanticize solutions. I'll do the next correct thing."

That got Valli's full smile, small and fleeting. "Good line," she said. "Keep it."

Vost's chin tipped, not quite a nod. "We're not done with this. We'll write the procedure addendum together, manual versus software decision tree. You're on it with me."

Aries blinked. "Me?"

"You touched it. You own it," she said. "Congratulations. It's yours forever."

Bennett clapped him on the shoulder and winced theatrically. "Welcome to adulthood."

THE TANKER UNDOCKED WITH A SHRUG. Time contracted. Checklists multiplied and died. On the flight deck, Rogers tuned the guidance like an instrument you could almost play by ear. CAPCOM's voice moved from ritual to rare as the local loop took priority.

"All stations, stand by for Trans-Mars Injection." Noah's voice filled the module, steady as the tide. "This is our ride. This is our window. Breathe and do your jobs."

Aries cinched his harness and tucked his gloved

fingers under the strap the way Skye had teased him was lucky. He looked left; Noah met his eyes. The nod exchanged between them was not forgiveness and not command. It was something sturdier.

"Ten seconds."

They lit the big engine and became a story about falling correctly. The burn was long and patient. Earth curved away; the arc opened, the Hohmann ellipse unfurling in math and heat. Six months on a highway that wasn't there yet, a line drawn between two moving targets. Primitive in concept, exquisite in practice.

Aries watched the numbers align: velocity change whispering up toward plan, propellant flow right on the slope, guidance making thousandths-of-a-degree prayers. He felt the acceleration as a hand on his chest, insistent but kind.

"Engine cutoff." Silence again, a new kind. The kind that meant commitment.

Reese's laugh was out before he could tuck it back. "We're on the arc."

"Course is perfect," Rogers said softly, because sometimes you were allowed that word.

Noah didn't speak right away. He let the crew hear the quiet. Then: "Six months," he said. "Everyone make a friend with time."

Aries let his head turn to the port. Earth had become a lovely, accusing marble. He didn't feel accused anymore. He felt connected by thread and gum wrapper, by hidden patch, by arguments worth having.

He thumbed his console and opened a private message he'd queued but did not send. — S.E.: We lit the sky. It stayed lit. He stared at it, then typed two more words: For luck. He didn't send it. He saved it. He liked the ritual.

Vost's voice cut across the cabin. "Karalis. After you drink and pee, you're with me and Valli on the decision tree. Then Reese wants you for the buffer tests."

Aries smiled into his helmet mic where only his father could hear. "Humanity's youngest unpaid intern."

Noah's reply was dry. "Interns don't touch pyros."

"Today they do," Aries said, and unbuckled into the long, exact work of outbound.

6

THE JOURNEY

The ship settled into the slow, unhurried arithmetic of a voyage. Outside the portholes, the stars slid by in patient arcs; within, life became a rhythm measured in routines and tiny rebellions against boredom.

For the first few days, every alarm and ping felt like an accusation, each sensor click a potential catastrophe waiting to happen. Then the systems found their cadence: scrubbers hummed, radiators sighed, gyros whispered corrections. The crew learned the spacecraft's peculiarities like a city's potholes and shortcuts. The initial adrenaline softened into steady, disciplined attention. If Mars was a promise, the transit was the long work of getting the promise to keep.

Noah and Aries established a rule in the second week: one hour each evening, no mission talk unless it was to say something important, no troubleshooting, no rehearsing failure. It would be a pocket of ordinary time carved out of an extraordinary life, one hour to be father and son, not commander and cadet.

They called it simply: the Hour.

Sometimes it was clumsy. Noah tried to teach Aries to tie a sailor's knot properly and wound a rope into an indecipherable skein. Aries mocked him gently and then fixed it more neatly than Noah could have imagined. Other nights they sat in the observation bubble with thermal mugs of reconstituted tea, and Noah told stories of his first nights on long-range sims, foolish bets won and lost over instant noodles and bad songs. Aries retaliated with meticulous diagrams of hypothetical habitation layouts, pointing out where Noah's old designs left life awkward.

"You plan for efficiency," Aries said one evening, eyes bright in the floating light. "You plan for function. But people are messy. We need a place that forgives being human."

Noah watched him, the lines at the corner of his

eyes softening. "You plan for the people," he said. "And you make the machines less lonely."

That became their shorthand. Heard in a dozen small ways: Aries would route an extra comm buffer for Noah's private channel; Noah would stop a drill and, instead of barking orders, ask Aries if he was eating enough, sleeping enough, if he'd forgiven himself for anything.

Their conversations shifted from guarded to grateful. Aries learned the strength of Noah's decisions: how he could balance risk, not by ignoring fear, but by categorizing it. Noah learned that his son's brilliance was more than rapid solutions; it was a hunger to understand, an empathy embedded inside math. He watched Aries correct a thermal model not with impatience but with a smile when he discovered a way to make a scrubber more human-safe.

They argued, of course, about protocols, about whether a certain fix was elegant enough to trust, about the meaning of grief. Those arguments never became wars; the Hour insulated them. When tempers flared, they would extract themselves, go to the observation bubble, breathe, and return with a truce so small it fit in the palm of a hand.

Outside those hours, Aries did what he had always done: he worked. He spent long stretches with Dr. Nate Reese refining comms buffers and building redundancy protocols that would tolerate a Martian dust storm and still whisper life back to Earth. He rewired handfuls of diagnostic rigs, turned his head to see where sensors lay, and fixed problems before they announced themselves.

On the quieter shifts, he retreated to the small sanctuary of his tablet and the voice that lived there, Eleni, or what he had left of her. The AI was a thinner thing than before, a voice he had pruned and a logic he had taught to stop answering questions he could not bear in full. He'd learned to prefer the clipped honesty of code to the messy, unfathomable warmth of human comfort when he was raw.

"Did you read the morning log?" he asked one night, voice low.

"You mean your sixteen-page analysis of scrubber variances? I have. You missed a comma on the pressure table," the AI replied, with the smallest echo of amusement. The inflection was his mother's, but slower, curated to be steadier.

"Fixing commas is one thing," he said. "Fixing

the part of me that thinks she left because of me —
that's another."

"There is no algorithm that resolves grief," the
voice said. "There is only tending: habits, routines,
truths you will tell yourself until they make a
different kind of sense."

Aries thumbed through a sequence he'd been
working on to tighten the cabin's CO_2 scrubber loop.
He spoke his thoughts aloud as much to hear them
organized as to hear the AI reflect them. Often the
conversation would loop into reprimand—gentle—
and then back into counsel. Sometimes he asked
Eleni things he knew she could not answer; sometimes it was enough for her to reframe the problem.

"You miss her," she said once, not as a diagnosis
but as a fact. "Good people leave marks. You carry
them, Aries. That is not failure."

He would end the dialog with a small ritual: he'd
simulate the smell of rain from a stored sample and
set the playback to fade with a lullaby file his mother
used to hum when he had fevers. It was tender and
ridiculous and exactly what he needed.

Skye's messages were different, electric, a thread
of human company that crossed the widening gulf
between ship and Earth. The delay grew as they

slipped farther from home, a few minutes at first and then a long, patient lag that turned the chat into an exchange of letters rather than conversation. She sent him sketches of Wave Three designs she was working on, voice notes about a broken servo she refused to fix until Aries told her a bad joke, photos of desert sunsets where the training towers blurred into the horizon. He answered with patches of code and the occasional smug technical win.

Their messages were both professional and personal. Skye mocked his habit of sewing contraband items into his collar, then sent a thumbnail of her own hidden talisman, a small rivet she'd taken from a broken rover and polished until it shone. He sent back a piece of his debug script annotated with doodles in the margins and emoticons, useless symbols for their shared language of practice and affection.

Once, while they were on a long transit burn and the ship's wake made a hush, Skye uploaded a short video of herself with a ribbon in her hair. "Cheer practice," she joked. "For when I see you again."

Aries watched it in the dim light of his bunk, thumb hovering over the reply. He typed and deleted and typed again. When he finally sent his message, it was simple:—S.E.: **Save a ribbon for me. I'll need a luck keeper.**

She replied an hour later with a grin and an image of a soldered ribbon with a small badge.—**S.E.: Already built.**

They were friends in the way of people who loved the same puzzles and the same jokes and who had learned to be tender across distance. The delay taught them patience; the content taught them endurance. Skye's voice, text, audio, images, became a lifeline back to Earth that didn't demand he carry its whole weight.

Not everything was easy. Twice they had small errors that set alarms wailing: a gas pocket strike that shook the outer radiator fins and sent thermal predictions swinging, a software race condition on the waste-recycling system that made the tanks sing like a kettle. Each time, Aries worked shoulder-to-shoulder with the systems officers, writing patches, unlatching valves, and listening more than speaking. He learned the value of a checklist recited like a prayer, the discipline of redundancy, the courage to hand a problem back to a tired colleague and trust them to do their part.

Those crises made the Hour more precious. Once, after a day spent lying awake monitoring a slow pressure bleed that turned out to be a faulty sensor, Noah found Aries in the observation bubble, eyes rimmed red.

"You held it together," Noah said softly, settling beside him without ceremony.

Aries shrugged. "I'm trying."

"Trying is not the same as pretending. You don't have to keep your face on just because people need you."

Aries looked at him. "You didn't go because you had to," he said, quieter. "But you stayed when it mattered tonight."

Noah's jaw worked. "I'll keep staying."

They sat with such civility until the stars blurred. Small promises accumulated into something like trust.

By the midpoint of the trip, the crew had its own physics of intimacy. People made habits: Vost snapping a particular stretch before an EVA simulation, Bennett humming to the thermal controls as he adjusted heat loads, Reese leaving little notes, links to new algorithms, taped near Aries's station.

The systems officers became not just safety nets but the closest thing to family the crew had on the highway to Mars.

Aries learned to accept compliments without

deflecting. Noah learned to ask for help and to take it. And both of them, in the quiet stitching of days, found the wound of loss becoming less of a raw thing to hide and more of a map to live by.

When the automated nav whispered the small joy of course corrections done and the tank gauges showed the slow satisfaction of fuel margins holding, Aries would send Skye a tiny note with a photograph of the engine bell glowing at dusk. He'd slip the image into his mother's AI folder afterward, as if to show her what they were doing, because on a voyage this long you wanted every witness you could carry.

They kept their Hour, even when a sleep schedule tried to collapse it to nothing. They found reasons, bad jokes, a shared attempt to make soup from rehydrated packets, a stubborn song Noah could never remember the lyrics to. They learned a new cadence for grief: not denial, not defeat, but an ongoing conversation.

Six months was long. It changed them, not with a single great event, but by its cumulative insistence: an argument remembered, a patch written at midnight, a laugh that started as a cough and became a smile. By the time the first blush of Mars touched the forward hull's sensors, the son and the man had learned to be teammates.

When the planet finally rose in the scope, ruddy and patient, they were not naïve. They were steadier. They had not forgotten or forgiven everything. They had instead practiced living with both things in their pockets. They had become better at the next correct thing.

7

SETTING UP THE BASE

The approach had been clean, textbook, six months of patient math and careful corrections, and now the red orb filled the forward displays with dust and promise. Ahead lay not only a landing zone mapped and re-mapped in simulations but a future to be laid down by careful cooperation.

Aries watched the planet grow large, and it started to hum with a kind of contained terror; everything that mattered was now small enough to touch. Noah's voice in his ear was quiet and exact: "Remember the sequence. Trust the checklist. Trust one another."

They came down in two maneuvers. The transfer stage burned and dropped away; the descent vehicle, sleek, squat, and bellied with equipment, slew in and bled velocity over the thin sky. Dust kicked into the sunlight in slow, angry puffs. Titan-X had done its work; the rest was theirs.

When their feet first found regolith, it felt more like a promise than an answer: a powder that felt like the future of life on Mars. The first boot to leave a print was Noah's, steady as a metronome, a perfect imprint on the crumbly dust. Aries did the same, smaller and sharp-edged. Vost's laugh, choked and bright, was the first human sound that was not procedural.

"We're a colony, not a platoon," Commander Karalis said into the radio, and someone somewhere on the ship laughed, steadying the sky.

The plan had been written in thousands of tiny, careful decisions: land, secure, pressurize, proliferate. The mission manifest prioritized seven critical infrastructures, power, shelter, life support, water and In Situation Resource Utilization, ISRU for short, communications, mobility & Exploration, food production, and a connective tissue of backup, automation, and people-procedures binding it all together. The first week would be violent with work.

The landing site, Eos Ridge, a flat plateau rimmed by basalt ridges and pocked with shallow impact basins, had been selected for its relative flatness, sun exposure, and the presence of a shallow aquifer signature detected by prior orbiters. The first task was to deploy the habitat cluster.

They unloaded the Modular Habitat Units (MHUs): four cylinders that snapped together like pieces of a greedy machine. Each MHU had its own function and redundancy: one for command and medical, one for crew living and galley, one for lab and manufacturing, and a sealed utility hub for scrubbers, water tanks and power buses. They rolled the first into place using rover-mounted actuators, massive fingers of aluminum and composite, and the team worked with the focused choreography of rehearsed dancers. Warnings were crisp and brief: a misalignment here could twist a seal and make a week of work become a disaster.

Dr. Yara Valli led the hull mating. She barked simple, precise orders. "Torque eight on the forward flank, not nine. Bennet, hold the thermal blanket; don't let the dust wedge." Her hands were sure, the scar over her eyebrow making a map Ari had memorized, lines that said *done*.

Aries spent that first morning tied into the diagnostics ring, his fingers tracing sensors while Noah oversaw the big picture. Noah anchored the team, but Aries was the one with the nimble mind for hidden bugs: a pressure sensor that reported in a different offset than the manual; a feed pump whose tolerance drooped in cold. He and Bennett worked a hiccup in the thermal routing, an insulation panel that had been compromised in transit. Bennett swore softly and then grinned. "You patch not only code, kid, you patch in the real world too."

By nightfall, with ammonia welders cooling and the first habitation cylindrical seams sealed, the crew harvested the small private miracle of artificial gravity inside a pressurized bubble. The first breath of recycled air tasted like triumph and lab polish.

Power came next, because nothing runs without it. The mission carried a hybrid system: a compact fission core for baseload and a generous array of foldable solar wings for peak and redundancy. The fission module, wrapped in layered shielding and industrial-sized cooling loops, went down first into a pre-dug trench. It hummed awake with a low, steady comfort. Bennett stood beside it with grease on his knuckles, and when the reactor bridged the bus, the lights across the camp came alive one at a time like blinking, careful stars.

"Power online," he said, and there was a small,

involuntary cheer from a knot of technicians who had been awake for twenty-seven hours.

Solar wings unfolded like giant metallic flowers and angled themselves toward the weak sun. They would harvest during the day; the reactor would shoulder the night. Power management was a jaw of complexity: surge buffers, battery banks, thermal control for cold nights, and a drive to avoid single points of failure. Rahul and Aries spent hours calibrating the power mesh, tuning the grid so scrubbers didn't drop when a rover started, so heaters cut in automatically when temperatures slumped and so the comms array never found the bus brownout.

"Don't forget the soft-start," Bennet reminded, thumb running through a field of amp draws. "If you chain the pumps, you'll trip the breakers."

Aries smiled. The soft-start was poetry. He threaded a small algorithm into the power controller that staggered boot sequences across the habitat cluster to reduce inrush. It shaved what could have been a messy cycle into a tidy rhythm.

Life support and atmospheric processing were the lungs. Dr. Evelyn Moreau and her team set up scrubbers, CO_2 reactors, humidity traps, and a labyrinthine plumbing of valves. The scrubbers used regenerative sorbent beds, cycling under careful timing to hold O_2 levels steady. The water system, ISRU's partner on this ride, was already busy: a mobile extractor unit rammed its scoops into the regolith at a few chosen sites, stirring up briny soils and pushing them through staged ovens to coax out bound water.

The water was raw and shy, salted with dissolved salt ions. Sophia Adamos' lab bench was a site for electrochemical reduction units, filters and small vials of pre-treated samples. The chemical dance was finicky; one test failed, and the filters clogged. Aries, elbow-deep in hose and sweat, helped design a pre-filter of polymer mesh that trapped the bulk particulates before the electrochemical cell. It worked. A small chorus of relieved expletives broke out, as if the machine's success felt like a load off.

Water was fed into the life support loop and the agricultural module. The hydroponics bay arrived as a box of hope. It was small and green as someone's first garden: trays of engineered regolith mixes, LED strips tuned to plant-appropriate spectra, and a slow-learning AI to manage nutrients. That first night, the seedlings were tiny arcs of life glowing under lamps, the first biological triumph whose value extended beyond calories. Dr. Moreau sat with her hands folded and watched the green with reverence for the life-giving substance they would be.

Food production would not feed the colony in the first weeks, but the psychological tonic it provided — lettuce, small herbs, the smell of something living — was invaluable. One of the assistants put an oregano plant into the hydroponic tray as a joke and then admitted, quiet-eyed, that she'd kept it alive because she liked the idea that something smaller than them could be stubborn and survive.

Mobility mattered. Chief Petty Officer Danika Vost took the rover fleet out across the rim and set up navigation beacons, little monoliths of steel and laser that etched a secure local trilateration grid. The rovers were both trucks and labs, equipped for cargo, trenching, and tethered power transfer. Trucks ran the first transects scouting basalt outcrops where radiation shielding by regolith would be easiest to engineer.

Structures and radiation protection were twin priorities. Dust was a thief here, abrading seals, fouling radiators, hiding in crevices. Valli set up buried berms and a simple regolith-mover: a scoop-and-pile technique to press a meter of soil over the living cluster. The first rammed shield held up the noon sun like a blanket; radiation readings fell into acceptably low ranges. They spent long, dirty days moving regolith by robot and hand, a choreography of machine and muscle. Aries would pilot a trenching arm one minute and trace a circuit the next; his hands learned both callus and precision.

EVA protocols hardened like cured epoxy. Danika drilled the crew on suit checks and emergency pressurization. "If you panic, you make mistakes," she said in her twang. "Fixations kill. The suit is your friend if you treat it like one."

Communications were the artery connecting the tiny human island to Earth. Dr. Nate Reese and his team erected a high-gain dish on a telescoped mast, calibrated steerable relay nodes, and stood up a local mesh network. The relay architecture used a low-latency buffer to Earth for non-critical telemetry and a prioritized shepherd for O_2 & CO_2 levels, power bus status, and life-critical diagnostics. The software stack had to be ruthlessly efficient; update packets were applied with surgical precision.

Reese sat with Aries, coding late-night scheduling algorithms that made sure telemetry windows matched both orbital passes and the human rhythm. "You can't just throw data at Earth," he said. "You have to whisper it so it can be heard."

Aries loved the whisper.

Manufacturing and repair were understated heroes: additive printers that could churn out brackets and specialized fittings, a small foundry that melded regolith-bonded composites for quick repairs, and a machine shop for tolerances mechanical minds still preferred. The lab module housed both biotech rigs and hardware printers. Aries led a team designing a quick-change mount for solar wing articulators after wind shear snagged one and misaligned its hinge. The fix was elegant and quick — an improvised spring and lock bolted on with a torque they whipped from the print queue. The solar arrays hummed again, a little crooked and still alive.

Redundancy and contingency planning threaded through every day. Every critical system had a fallback. If the reactor hiccupped, the solar wings and battery banks could hold vital loads for days. If comms went dark, the local mesh could run the life support's automated calls. If a rover was lost, its tools were designed to be removable and re-mounted on a replacement. Procedures were written and then rewritten under stress.

Training remained constant. New challenges spawned new checklists. The colonists practiced rapid isolation of an infected module, the slow and patient task of removing salt contamination from a water feed, the elegant brutality of triage when time was not on anyone's side.

The human side of infrastructure was less tangible but no less essential. Governance was provisional and pragmatic: a rotating council drawn from the systems officers and crew leads with Noah as mission commander, and a lightweight charter that prioritized survival, equal access to resources, and a hard rule to make kindness a metric. They institutionalized a twice-daily check-in, short, uncensored time for members to speak freely of their fears, or concerns. Dr. Sierra had taught them the breathwork and the practice of "presence minutes," small rituals to root people into the now.

Culture had to be built as deliberately as any power bus. They staged an opening night with reconstituted meals that tasted like home, and a small, badly performed play written by the hydroponics team. Laughter ricocheted between walls with the same sweet absurdity as a campfire joke.

Religion, art, music — they arrived by slow degrees. Aries built a small shrine of things that mattered: the rocket model from his mother, Skye's gum, a secret patch that was stitched into his collar. People left small offerings at the communal table —

a stone, a scrubbed fossil, a bad pencil drawing, things that said, "I was here."

Not everything went well. A week in, a late-night microfracture appeared on one of the habitat seals. The morning found the seam letting in a hairline leak that would have become catastrophic if not caught. Valli's hands moved like a surgeon; Moreau hunched over the pressure graphs; Bennett patched a thermal shunt. They instituted a stopgap seal and recommissioned a backup habitat compartment as spare. The fix cost time and sleep, and it reminded them all the planet didn't negotiate.

There were small bodies of grief, too. A loaf of bread that didn't rise. A failed potato crop that tasted like ash. A radio message from Earth that had been mis-routed and came late with a funeral they had no power to attend. The colony learned rituals for passing through these small storms: a bell that someone rang when a failure was significant enough to note, a gathering where people told stories about what they had lost and what they had learned.

By the end of the first month, the skeletal structures were up, and the numbers that mattered were stable: oxygen within safe margins, water at sustainable production rates, power comfortably supporting the cluster, comms reliably reaching relay with a lag but no blackouts. The rover grid extended in spokes from the habitat, and the first geological cores were bagged and cataloged. The colony had a rhythm.

Aries and Noah found time to walk the berms they had built, to touch the packed soil and test its compaction. They spoke, sometimes in short sentences, sometimes in tones that unraveled into laughter. The Hour remained, now less about granting themselves a break than about remembering why they had built this: not just to survive, but to make a place where people could be human.

One evening, standing on the edge of their first buried shield, watching the sun sink into a pale horizon and the long, slow planet exhale, Aries felt a small, remarkable thing: not completeness, but the right kind of incompleteness. They had made a beginning. The colony breathed under its layered crust of electronics and care.

No one pretended it was finished. They called it quietly, a little fiercely, the first honest house in a new world.

"Dad," Aries said, voice small against the vastness, "We did it. Your Dream. We actually did it."

Noah's hand was warm on his shoulder. "We

started it," he corrected. "You did more than you know."

They stood there for a while, and listened to life, pumps, a distant solar pivot, the quiet scrape of a rover crossing a regolith, and knew, for the first time in a long time, that the next correct thing had been done. The rest would be learned one long, stubborn hour at a time.

8

ROUTINE AND ORDER

By the time the colony settled into its second season, the extraordinary had become a series of ordinary miracles, the steady hiss of scrubbers, the soft thunk of rover wheels packing new trails, the ritual clink of cups as people learned to drink like citizens of two worlds. The work no longer had the frenzied edge of survival; it had the patient geometry of maintenance and improvement. There was time to plan small comforts.

Aries built his with his hands and a mind that refused to stop asking questions.

He assembled the pod from a spare habitat cylinder that had been decommissioned after the seal fracture. Valli had declared it structurally sound if you did your math right and your torque even, which Aries did. He lined the inner ribs with a second skin of composite panels, threaded the little airlock with a double-gasket, and fed its heart with a tap off the secondary life-support loop so the pod could breathe without robbing the main. It would be a luxury by colony standards: not essential, not a piece of infrastructure the council could point to on a bar graph. It was instead a place for one human to sit and talk to the memory of his mother.

Inside, he built the interface, the thing he'd been half-assembling for months: a thin holo-array that could render his mother's face in soft resolution from the archived footage and the voice models he'd painstakingly tuned. He had promised himself he wouldn't build her face again; but he had also promised that he would keep her present for himself in ways that felt honest. The pod's visuals were not a trick to replace grief. They were a window. He set the rendering to a dim warmth and taught it to smile carefully, to blink with a rhythm his mother had once used when she was thinking.

He called the pod Luna, because it was small and gave him comfort like the moon did on Earth.

Skye's messages reached him in the small hours and in long-delayed bursts. She was still earth-bound, Wave Three waiting its slow bureaucratic turn, chatting in half-letters about the things that mattered on the planet below: a new torque she'd redesigned for a solar hinge, a moonrise over a training field that looked almost like a bruise. When she sent video, the latency stretched their jokes into patient, funny letters. They traded pieces of code and songs and the ridiculous details of human life that didn't fit in a checklist.

"Show me the view," she demanded in one message one week, and Aries remotely repositioned the pod's external cam, angling it so she could see the nearest ridge and the way the light folded over the crushed crust.

She responded with a video of a rainstorm in a backyard on Earth, the drops cartoonishly large in the sheen on a parked car. They both laughed at the absurdity of the wet brightness.

Life in the colony had become a negotiation. Routine was comforting, but routine also meant steady stress: who controlled the water banks when demand spiked? Who decided which rover got priority to a newly-discovered outcrop? Systems officers sat on the council in rotation, and their egos, carefully tempered by the demands of survival, still had teeth.

Small conflicts flared into sharp, practical debates. Moreau insisted on a conservative cycle for scrubber regeneration to avoid sorbent stress; Bennett argued that a tighter stagger would allow more power to be diverted to the manufacturing presses. Valli wanted to divert a rover to shore up a weak berm; Vost argued the rover's scheduled maintenance made that impossible without risking mobility.

The council meetings were ugly and beautiful at once, technical arguments masquerading as morality plays. Procedures were adjusted in real time: a layered priority matrix was written with Valli's hands and Bennett's calculations, with compromise clauses that read like negotiated treaties. "We will not let systems become fiefdoms," Noah said one night. "Nobody gets absolute control. We will build bridges, not barricades."

The statement was gentler than a command; it was meant to say that power here had to be shared because the planet did not care for proprietorship. The systems officers grunted and wrote the matrix into the ledger. For all their competence, the colonists needed one another's goodwill like they needed air.

Aries watched much of this from the observation

rim or from the pod. He learned something about leadership that textbooks could not teach him: people kept trust by showing each other the seams. When a system failed, the person who owned it brought both the complaint and the solution; when a suggestion came from someone young and loud, the elders tested it, not dismissed it. The colony became an organism that thrived on the willingness to be wrong in public.

One afternoon, with dust like powdered iron slung across the horizon and the distant sun filtering through it, Noah found him in the pod. He walked in wearing the sort of calm that came from a man who knew the cost of being angry with his son.

"You've built a good place here," Noah said, his voice low in the narrow room.

Aries watched the holo-face of his mother blink in the corner, the laugh lines he'd taught it to keep, then shut the rendering down with a practiced motion. Even in a small room, there were ceremonies.

"You could've used that cylinder for stores," Noah said. "For spares."

"I built it because I wanted to ask her things, Dad," Aries replied. "Because when I talk to her, I don't have to pause as much. She listens until I can make the sentence finish itself."

Noah sat on the single cot, the fabric sighing under him. "I thought about doing the same," he said. "But I was afraid. That it would be too real. That I'd ..." His sentence smoothed out. "That it would be a way to keep her absent when she's not."

Aries surprised himself by reaching out, touching the worn patch stitched into his collar where his mother's thread still pulsed like a secret. "I wanted you to have her," he said. "Not as a replacement. Just..." He searched for the right smallness of phrasing. "...like an offering."

Noah's eyes shone. He folded his hands. "You want me to have her? Really?"

Aries nodded and, with the deliberate awkwardness of a kid who had learned to do delicate things clumsily, he copied the filesystem. He handed Noah a card — small, heat-wrapped, a physical token that contained the AI's voice model and a visual pack. It was not a perfect archive, he'd compartmentalized it to avoid scenes that would hurt until he was ready to process them, but it held the cadence of her laugh, the way she asked follow-up questions, the ways she had answered when he was seven and afraid of thunder.

Noah took the card with hands that trembled and, for a moment, the commander and the father separated and the father moved to the center. He slid the card into a reader, and the pod filled softly, almost imperceptibly, with the sound of her saying his name.

"Hello, Noah," the voice said, his mother's voice, gentled into a cadence the AI had learned, then softened again to suit him.

Noah exhaled. He spoke into the quiet. "Eleni?"

The AI blinked in its own way and replied with the old humor, "You missed lunch, honey."

They stood with the sound between them, two people who had found a way to fold a vanishing into something near enough to touch. It was not tidy. It was not final. It was an allowance.

That night, the colony shimmered in the way that places do when people feel seen. The walls hummed. The hydroponics bay glowed green. Rovers traced new maps. Somewhere outside, a low wind unrolled like a slow ocean and carried dust in little curling eddies that made the light itself look sifted.

A week later, disputes again threatened to fray the tight web of cooperation. A newly-found thin vein of ice in a shallow basin offered a dramatic improvement in water yield, but it lay midway between two outposts and required a dedicated pipeline to secure. Valli argued the engineering case: it could be extracted safely with a small trench and insulated line. Moreau argued about epidemiological risk: disturbing the deposit could raise aerosols that would stress scrubbers. Bennett saw the numbers and performed arithmetic like a man praying.

Noah called an open forum. People brought models, charts, arguments, and fears. Voices rose. For an hour it looked ugly, pride carving its claim, expertise flexing its muscle. Then, as fatigue settled like dust, something quieter crept in: people began to offer trade-offs. Valli volunteered a phased extraction plan; Moreau negotiated additional pre-filters designed with Aries and Bennett to manage aerosols; Vost offered to station one rover as a shuttle and a safety fallback. The plan that emerged was not any one person's victory; it was a stitched compromise that made the colony stronger.

"People make places livable, not technologies," Noah said afterward, repeating the lesson like a mantra. "We pick a planet and we carry our patches. That's the work."

Aries watched his father then with a new tenderness. He saw how Noah listened, really listened, when the stakes were human and not just technical. He watched his father give ground where it mattered and stand firm where it needed holding. He realized in a small, blunt way that forgiveness was sometimes less a single moment than practice, a pattern repeated until it became easier to repeat it again.

On a slow evening, Aries and Noah walked the ridge outside the berm. The view was a high one: an ocean of broken red, the plains fractured by long shadowed gullies, distant hills like cut velvet. The sky at that hour was a washed lapis darkening to ink, and in that light, Mars looked both ancient and newly minted: a world that had been waiting for human stubbornness like a patient host.

Noah's voice came a shaky, a little awed by the view, "I still can't believe I am here".

"Truly a dream come true," he said. "But never in my dreams was it this perfect."

Aries breathed in the air in his helmet in a way that felt ceremonial. He let the planet imprint. He let the grief settle into the background of his ribs.

Noah turned to him. "I'm sorry," he said again, and his voice was thinner, more precise. "For not being there when she left. I was..." He paused and found the simpler shape of the truth. "I was afraid I couldn't hold both the mission and her. I was wrong."

Aries felt the old anger, the small, hot shrapnel, soften. He could still feel it, but the edges no longer jabbed at him the same way. "I'm sorry for calling you cold," he said. "I was grieving and had the wrong target."

They looked at one another like two mechanics who had learned how to pass a wrench without arguing over grip. They didn't erase the past. They set it down somewhere safer.

"You're my father," Aries said. "You taught me to build things that hold. Teach me how to hold the people I love too."

Noah's hand closed over his shoulder, firm. "I'll teach you. And you teach me to ask for help the right way."

They laughed, the sound small and close, and then quieted. The wind moved a little, lifting a sleeve of dust and sending it skittering like a living thing.

Before they turned back to the berm and the small habitats that were stitched together from foam and metal and stubborn hearts, Aries pulled Noah aside. He reached into his utility pocket and produced another card, the same file set he had given in the pod earlier, but this one updated, paired with a father's preferences and a son's tenderness. "For when you want to talk," he said. "When you don't want to wake the whole habitat."

Noah took it. His fingers were steady this time. He tucked the card into a reader on his wrist and, after a breath, the tiny speaker whispered his wife's voice like a folded letter. He closed his eyes. "Thank you," he said, as a small confession.

On the walk back, the colony glowed behind them, windows alight, the solar petals catching the last of the sun, each light a small promise kept. The future here would not be easy. It would not be clean. But they had, between them, stitched enough trust to keep trying.

When Aries leaned against the berm and watched the stars come on one by one, he felt, for the first time in a long time, that the next correct thing was not simply a cold decision. It was a choice you practiced every morning and evening, in small mercies and small truths, until the orbit of your life moved truer.

Commander Noah Karalis liked two things about meals: that they were predictable, and that they forced people to look up from screens and each other's workloads. He'd instituted the communal dinner within the first week, no exceptions unless the person was literally dying. He called it the anchor, and said it like a man who had rehearsed metaphors until they sounded true.

"Food shared is a problem halved," he told them on the second night, shaping an old proverb to fit a new planet, and, somehow, it stuck.

Tonight the galley smelled like something between toasted grain and Earth cheer, rehydrated stew with a mysterious spice packet Skye had snuck into his bag swearing would "taste like home," and a pan of flatbreads browned the way Bennett liked them: too dark by consensus, perfect by his standards. The hydroponics bay had donated basil that smelled shockingly alive.

They gathered at the long table that had been bolted into the habitat like a communal spine. Thirty faces, different histories. Thirty small stories stacked into this one makeshift planet.

Noah stood at the head, sleeves rolled. "Five minutes," he said. "Then we eat."

People finished last-minute tasks — a soldering iron tucked away, a data pad snatched into a pocket, an untamed mass of hair tied up to keep it back. The table filled in the natural order of their micro-society: systems officers at one side like elders, trainees scattered, the crew leads clustered near the commander.

The first spoonfuls of stew passed hands like an offering. Forks and spoons made soft music against the ration-grade bowls.

Dr. Evelyn Moreau spooned carefully, the motion precise and unobtrusive. "We're within the recommended humidity variance," she announced between chews, which had become her way of landing a technical point without waiting for a meeting. "Keeping the scrubber cycles steady and staggering the laundry drying."

"Laundry is a war I will not fight tonight," muttered Chief Roger Bennett, lifting his bowl like it was a chalice. He had grease on his knuckles from hours ago and a grin that made the others forgive him preemptively. "We are at nominal power. I say extra flatbreads are justified."

Lieutenant James Rogers, who ate like a man who had known many hard landings and preferred his calories without drama, nodded. "Nominal is the word I like. I also prefer my carbs toasted."

Dr. Yara Valli took a large bite and then cut to the point. "We'll need to reroute one rover for berm maintenance tomorrow morning. Danika, you can have the second watch."

Danika Vost didn't look up from her plate. "I will take it if the rover's filters have been swapped. I don't babysit contaminated hardware, only humans."

"Then someone will need to make the filters," said Moreau. Two hands lifted to volunteer: a young systems tech whose name badge read Mira and a soft-spoken mechanic named Ephraim. The volunteering felt like a small warmth passing across the table.

Aries noticed, as always, small details, the way people's hands moved when they were relaxed, the tilt of eyes when they lied to be polite. He liked watching the crew, the same way he liked watching code run: predictable, readable, but with beautiful exceptions.

Dr. Sophia Adamos, who believed in the healing power of food as much as lab sterilization, piped up between mouthfuls. "The crew needs vitamins. We're replacing fresh calories slowly, but we're already seeing better sleep cycles in people who are eating together and not alone."

Noah watched them all with a look that softened his stony features. "Eat, then talk," he said. "We'll do operations notes afterward. If anyone wants privacy for a call, take it. But come back for dessert."

Dessert in Colony terms was usually a thin square of reconstituted chocolate or a shared bowl of rehydrated fruit. Tonight it was a simple affair — slices of preserved mango that skated the line between cheerful and sweet. The table treated them like a forbidden delicacy.

Conversation folded and refolded along technical and trivial lines. Valli told a story about a stubborn hinge that had almost taken her head off in a simulator; she told it with a grin that suggested she intended to do it again sooner than later. Vost rolled her eyes but laughed; Moreau pretended not to hear, the way elders pretend not to be soft.

Aries made time to talk to Skye. "Are you and your dad doing well?" she asked Aries quietly.

"We are trying," he said.

"Do you speak to your mom often?" she asked, and the question was gentle as a probe.

He nodded. "I visit the pod at night. I think more clearly with it on." His voice was small but honest. "It's not perfect." He shrugged, embarrassed that his confession felt like a vulnerability he hadn't practiced.

"It's not supposed to be perfect," Skye said. "It's a mirror that helps you practice conversation."

Skye's screen blinked again. She'd recorded another short clip, this one showing her polishing a small rivet with concentration and devotion. "Offer for barter," she promised. "I will bring you a ridiculous charm when I get my turn."

LATER, when the technical parts of the evening began, Noah stood and cleared his throat the way he did when he wanted to steer the group. The mechanical noise of the habitat faded — lids closing, cups clinking, the soft hum of scrubbers — and attention tilted his way.

"Two items," he said. "One: the pipeline to the new ice vein is approved under Valli's phased plan. Two: cultural reminder, we eat together not because I like standing up here but because shared time keeps things real. When we skip meals, we drift. We want us to be a people building a place for other people, not a sealed experiment."

Murmurs of agreement came. It wasn't just Noah's word; it was a practice they'd all bought into. They'd learned how easy it was to become an island in a colony.

The conversation heated briefly over allocation: whether the hydroponics bay's next tray should be herbs or a small grain experiment. Bennett wanted grain; Moreau wanted leafy greens for oxygen; Aries lobbied for a mixed-rotation that optimized both. Each argued with the gentle ferocity of people who had learned that survival was a complicated math of many human needs.

"You always make the right choice," Skye's delayed voice said, saved for when the clip unspooled.

Valli looked at Aries. "You think you can keep the rotation going and still do your comms patches?"

"I can," he said. "I have a script that will run the comms sweep at dawn."

Valli snorted, the sound almost identical to laughter. "You little machine."

For a minute, between the jokes and the technical jargon and the small human boasts, the table felt like the heart of something that could keep beating.

LATER STILL, when bowls were cleared and messages buffered onto personal tabs, people lingered. Some wanted a second cup of whatever-passable-tea the galley offered. Others drifted toward the window to look out at the world that was now their horizon: red, fluted, and impossibly beautiful.

Noah watched his son, and then the crew. He next watched the planet and felt, noticeably, a kind of pride. He walked over to Aries and put a hand on his shoulder, in a motion that had the weight of a man who had learned to be gentle with the people he loved.

"You did well tonight," he said, not loudly, just there in the soft after-light.

Aries looked up, not quite ready to say anything grand. "We did it," he said.

Noah's smile was small and honest. "These meals are good for the group," he said. "For they help temper the arguments, and the mornings that we may not be able to bear."

Aries felt the truth of that in his chest. Mealtime was a connection. It kept the colony human.

THE REST of the night slid toward ritual: small repair teams hoisted a crate to the maintenance bay, a couple of engineers argued about the best placement for a sensor array and lost that argument to a consensus that felt oddly fair, and a trio of juniors sat in a corner teaching each other a slurred, triumphant song about the first time they'd cooked rice that didn't come out like glue.

Skye's buffered video had one last cut, an image of her tucking a ribbon into a tiny pouch, the ribbon smoothed and folded with care. She held it up and mouthed a quiet, lagged message: "for luck."

Aries watched it and then drew his hand to his heart, where the hidden patch lay like a small, private promise. He felt the table. He felt the patch of human time they were making every night. He felt that, with all the machines and maps and hard rules of physics, what they were building would not survive if it were only metal. It needed people who ate together, who quarreled and made up, who bartered goofy charms and recipes like currency.

Commander Karalis's dinner hour did more than feed bellies. It fed the colony's soul. It kept their arguments honest, their grief shared and therefore lighter. It let them be people in the middle of an impossible job.

When the watchers dimmed their stations and the scrubbers hissed into their nighttime cycles, the lights above the long table dimmed too, a small, human nightfall. People drifted back to bunks and watch schedules and quiet tasks. The last to leave the table tidied the bowls and stacked them, a practiced motion like the closing of a book.

Aries stayed a moment longer and then, with a young tenderness and a certain studied awkwardness, rose to gather the bowls. He stacked them carefully, lining rims with the care of someone who knew a lot of things could be fixed if you were willing to start with small, right actions.

He walked out of the galley into the cool, bruised air of the airlock. He was headed for Luna to tell his mom good night as the colony hummed, in their small habitat on a world that had not asked for them, but that received them anyway.

9

NIGHT FALLS

A ries retreated to Luna, the narrow cylinder tucked like a secret into the eastern row of the greenhouse quarter. The polished tube with a small round hatch and a window looked straight into a wall of lettuce. Once inside, the world around him faded away. It was the only place he could talk privately to his mother without feeling like he was disturbing the colony's sleep.

He crawled in, belly to metal, the way a kid might crawl under a porch to feel the world a little different. The hatch shut with a padded click. He thumbed the internal lights to amber and the holo-array to dim. The interface eye, his tiny, cautious camera, woke with a muted blink.

"Hi, Mom," he said. The speaker — a flat square he'd built into the wall — answered with a rustle of digital breath.

"Hi, kid," she said, her voice like warm paper. He had tuned her down over time, traded fidelity for mercy. What remained were cadences and choices, the comfort of her questions. He stretched, socked feet nudging the tube's far end, and watched the lettuce sway beyond the little viewport. He told her about the day: the pipeline compromise, a grumpy hinge, the basil that tasted like victory. He left out the way his chest had hurt for a moment when the sun hit the solar petals just right and he thought of rain on a car hood.

The AI Elani asked the gentle questions that made him sort himself: "Did you eat more than your ration today?" "Did you ask for help before you needed it?" "What will be different tomorrow because of what you learned?"

He answered honestly, because lying to a program was like lying to a mirror.

Outside, the greenhouse's LED strips dimmed into their night cycle, slipping from bright work-white to a low constellation. Somewhere down the row, a pump knocked and then settled. In the habitat ring beyond the greenhouse, the dinner crowd broke into watch schedules and bunk rituals and the familiar hush of thirty people agreeing to let each other rest.

He steered the conversation into the soft places he didn't show many others. With the tired guilt that still sparked at odd hours, she had gone out into the storm for him; he had kept living anyway. The sharp joy that came like a theft when Skye made him laugh. The way his anger at Dad had become something else, less a weapon than a vocabulary he and his father were learning to speak with fewer sharp edges.

"Grief moves at its own speed," the AI said once, an insight he knew he had written and then forgotten. "Thin air, sudden storms, long flats where you think nothing is moving until you see, in the corner of your eye, a shadow that wasn't there yesterday."

He smiled at that, unguarded. "That one was good," he admitted. "We should save it."

"We save everything," she teased gently.

"You hoarder," he teased.

He yawned, the kind that starts in the bones. The tube's warmth, the plant-breath, the after-dinner quiet did a trick on his body clock. He told himself he'd head back to the bunk in ten minutes. He shifted to his side, pulled the spare blanket over his shoulder, and let the AI's voice curl around him.

"Set light to dawn in ninety," he murmured, half-asleep.

"Okay," she said, fond and automatic, and dimmed even further. The pod's little fan purred. Leaves moved in slow-motion silhouettes. Somewhere far, the habitat's thermal panels creaked as they shed the last of the day's heat.

Aries slept like a child who trusted his house.

At 1:00 local, the habitat's systems accepted an over-the-air update to the environmental controller. Vost had scheduled it — routine, minor, a patch to reduce false-positive O_2 surge alarms when someone opened an airlock too quickly. It had tested clean in the sim tank. The patch included a new sleep mode for off-shift hours: a power-saving feature that staggered non-critical loads, put heaters into float, reduced scrubber cycle rates, and, unbeknownst to anyone because a single line had been mis-flagged, temporarily disabled the O_2 low alarm while the controller recalibrated its thresholds.

At 1:09, the update rolled across the bus. The heaters dipped to float. The scrubbers slowed and then idled. The alarm code set a flag to mute and then waited for a reset event that never arrived, because the condition it was built to catch now looked like its own maintenance window. The watchdog process, meant to bark if anything stayed muted longer than thirty seconds, had been pointed by mistake to the wrong memory address, an old buffer left over from a diagnostic harness Aries himself had written during transit and then removed. The watchdog watched an empty room and reported it quiet.

At 1:37, cabin CO_2 levels rose above baseline. No beep. At 1:59, condensation crawled on the inside of one porthole as the partial pressure shifted and the temperature slid. Sleepers turned in their bunks; someone muttered in a dream; someone else sighed. At 2:18, a junior tech on night watch pulled a blanket higher, thinking of Earth, and drifted.

At 2:51, the heaters slipped another half-degree. Frost began to feather the shadow edges in the equipment bay. At 3:04, a trainee's breath slowed, brain misreading the heavy air as sleep. At 3:30, the quiet was complete.

No alarms. No struggle. The house exhaled and did not inhale.

In Luna, the tube had its own micro-loop, a trick of design: Aries had tapped it into the secondary life support bus with a check-valve and, greedy and careful, had plumbed a small rebreather in line with the greenhouse's own O_2 bump, tiny, enough to keep seedlings sweet during night cycles. The plants kept breathing slowly; the tube's little fan kept shuffling a pocket of acceptable air. He slept on, a boy in a pipe, held alive by lettuce and his own fussiness.

He woke to the cold first: the kind that kisses lips and fingers and makes you bring your hands under your shirt. The amber lights had brightened toward a fake dawn. He blinked, momentarily content with the smallness of the tube, the low drone of the fan, the soft aftertaste of basil on the air.

"Mom?" he whispered.

"I'm here," the AI Elani said, and in the way the words fell, he heard nothing wrong. Habit made him check the time. 6:12. He grimaced, knowing he'd be catching looks for missing the early exercise cycle. He rubbed his eyes. "Okay. Back to the world."

He popped the hatch.

Light bled in faster than his eyes could widen. The greenhouse beyond was a dream of life. The LEDs were on their morning light cycle.

"Check the ring, check the ring," he muttered. He put on his helmet, and trotted lightly, careful to keep his head from ringing in the airlock. Aries ran across the colony to the Habitat, jumping into the airlock. Sensing something was wrong, he left his helmet on.

The Habitat's main corridor was quiet in a way that his mind started to try to understand it. Quiet, not good quiet, not a pulled-plug quiet either; the quiet of a house that has decided not to wake up. He tried comms. "Reese, you on?" Nothing but the soft hiss of his own channel. His fingers went to the rail, sliding him quickly around the curve to the galley.

He saw the first body slumped in a chair, and the child part of his brain said asleep, and the engineer side knew better. Two bowls unwashed, a spoon tipped. A hand reaching without urgency. He didn't touch, didn't shake; he knew enough about dignity and last postures to leave them a second untouched.

His breath came faster. The heaviness in his head tightened. He opened his mouth and pulled air like you do underwater. It didn't help.

"Alarm," he said, to the room, to the controllers, to the absent sensors. Nothing. The O2 low light over the galley door sat dark, dumb as a dead eye.

He ran. He knew exactly where to go.

The environmental panel in Utility hummed the way the wrong song played at the right volume hums, fine if you weren't listening; unbearable if you were. The screen reported routine maintenance. He swore a word he'd learned from Vost and pulled up the daemon log.

The code fell open like a murder scene. If he had been another person, he would have cried first; because he was who he was, he traced the chain with fingers already moving toward a fix.

"Update at 1:03, flag set, mute the alarms..." He exhaled a laugh that sounded like choking. "Of course. Of course I left you there."

His own diagnostic buffer, old, orphaned, waved at him from a corner of the log with stupid, cheerful innocence. He swore again and forced the watchdog to point home. He killed the maintenance flag with a code change. He spooled the scrubber cycle into forced mode and told the heaters to wake up like they'd been called by name.

Fans spun. Deep somewhere, the scrubbers clicked and engaged. The house took a breath, then ran on triumphantly. Warmth nudged. The O_2 low alarm blinked, realized it had been gagged, and screamed to make up for lost time. He silenced it gently, the way you hush a child in a church.

He stood with his hand on the panel and counted: in for four, hold for seven, out for eight. Training wrapped around panic like gauze.

Then he ran again.

He moved through the ring with work in his hands, the kind of work that had nothing left to save but demanded doing. He shut his eyes in doorways and opened them anyway. He turned bodies gently, checking for the rare miracle of breath. He blocked two alcoves with blankets because the cold made silhouettes look like hope.

He didn't call names. The symptom he and Dr. Sierra had once discussed, naming as you lose, felt like a cruelty here. He counted instead: one, two, three...

"Oh no, not again, Dad." Aries ran.

He found his father in the bunks, head on the pillow, expression calm, the laugh lines softened into something that looked like a nap. Noah's hand was open on the blanket, palm up, and in it lay the tiny reader card Aries had made him. His wrist unit showed a power dip at 2:52.

Aries sat. His throat narrowed and held. He didn't move Noah's body, didn't tidy it, not yet. He touched the card. "I hope you can talk to her now," he said to the room, to the man, to the ghost.

He waited for the part where he screamed or broke the way pamphlets promised that you would. Instead, a clarity arrived that felt like someone opening a window in his head. There would be time to howl. There wasn't now.

He did what he had been trained to do by a planet that punished delay: he thought to treat the living. There weren't any.

The heaviness in his chest eased with the scrubbers' second cycle; his brain warmed. The house continued to wake.

He went back to Utility and wrote the patch he would trust to keep the house from killing whoever came next: he removed the maintenance mute entirely, made the alarm idiot-proof, and added a second independent alarm on a simple circuit that didn't care what the system thought. He pushed the correction to every controller, then printed the change log on paper and taped it to the panel like a warning for a future self who might be tired and forgetful.

He returned to Noah's bunk. He sat there for a moment. He touched the sheet as if it might say something back. The room smelled faintly metallic, a ghost of cold and iron. He stared at his father's open hand and set his palm into it briefly, like an old ritual. Then he took the card, because if he left it, the card would feel lost.

He went to the galley.

Mealtime would not come again for a while. He knew he had to move the bodies, eventually. He knew the cold would come back at night if he mismanaged power. He knew he had to call Earth.

He set the AI card on the table gently. He brewed tea because his hands needed something to do that didn't involve triage. The kettle clicked. The sound made him cry finally — determined tears that realized what his mind tried to block. He let them run and felt them stop all by themselves, like a son who didn't have any tears left.

He wiped his face, took his tablet, and brought up a message to Mission Control. The link when it opened felt like an old friend knocking. He typed first: Emergency. All hands down. Environmental controller update caused CO_2 scrubber shutdown and the O_2 alarms to be disabled. Heaters cycled off. The entire crew is unresponsive. I am the only one alive due to an isolated loop in Greenhouse Quarter.

Then he forced himself to speak, and his voice was steadier than he thought it would be.

"Mission Control, Wave One, Karalis Aries, Systems Cadet," he began, defaulting to rank because the formality kept the grief from blowing the roof off his mouth. "At approximately zero one zero three local, an update to the enviro system initiated maintenance mute, set heaters to off, reduced scrubber cycles, and disabled O_2 low alarm pending recalibration. No alarms sounded. I woke at zero six twelve in the greenhouse quarter. I found elevated CO_2, low temp, and multiple unresponsive crew in the habitat. I've rolled back the mute, repointed the alarm, forced scrubbers to high, and brought heaters back. I've installed a hardware interlock and an independent CO_2 bell with no software dependency. The house is breathing again. The colony is not."

He paused, swallowed, and continued. "Commander Noah Karalis is deceased. Dr. Moreau, Dr. Valli, Chief Vost, Dr. Reese, Dr. Adamos, Lieutenant Rogers, Chief Bennett..." he couldn't make himself say all the names and knew he would have to later, "... all personnel appear to have passed in sleep. There were no signs of distress."

He breathed once, in and out, and made his voice a little more human. "I'm alone."

He sent the packet, voice, log attachments, photos of the panel and the bodies he had not framed as bodies so much as facts. He watched the data spool to send; it would take minutes to Earth and longer yet to come back. He did the math of delay; he knew how much time he had to live with the first reply's absence.

He stood. The house hummed, returning to its chores. He felt the scrubbers' rhythm now like a second pulse in the walls. He thought of the tube, Luna, in the greenhouse and thought of crawling back inside the one place where the air was reliable. He didn't move. He cleaned the galley instead, because it was work his hands understood: stacked bowls, wiped a table, arranged spoons. He gathered blankets. He found a simple sheet of paper and wrote, with the stubborn neatness of a kid doing his first penmanship drills: DO NOT UPDATE. PATCH IN PLACE. CALL BEFORE TOUCHING THIS.

He taped it to the door. He stood at the threshold and listened. Somewhere, a pump cycled. Somewhere, the greenhouse leaves rustled. Somewhere in his chest, something old and sharp poked its head up again. Aries cried in his helmet.

He went back to Noah. He sat again. He set the AI card gently on the pillow and, for the first time since opening the hatch of Luna, spoke not to the house or to Earth but to the woman whose voice he had built and to the man whose hand was now cool and still.

"We started it, Dad," he whispered. "I'll keep it going, I promise. I'm sorry that I wasn't there for you. I'm not leaving; I will build your dream."

He did not know yet what rituals would make sense in a house of one. He knew already that he would keep the Hour, time to talk to his Dad. He would talk in Luna to his mom until the plants got sick of him. He would answer Skye's queued messages when they arrived. He would wait for Mission Control's reply, and in the waiting he would become something he had not wanted to practice: the first citizen of a city that was suddenly too big for one.

He stood. He breathed. He made the next correct thing happen: he walked the ring and checked the panel and then checked it again. He turned on the CO_2 bell just to hear it ring, loud, ugly, impossible to ignore, and then turned it off with a hand that did not shake.

OUTSIDE, the sky lifted its pale sun. The ridge threw long shadows across the berm. The solar petals angled themselves politely into the morning. The planet, as always, was vastly indifferent and unbearably beautiful.

Luna waited, a little room with a voice inside. The house breathed. Aries did too. He opened a new log. He wrote: Day One.

10

RECKONING

A ries Karalis had never known silence like this. Mars, once buzzing with thirty voices, laughter over meals, arguments over systems, Commander Karalis's sharp orders echoing in the habitat corridors, was now mute. Every footstep Aries made sounded like an intrusion. Every door hiss felt like an accusation. And every breath — ragged, shallow, then steadier as the scrubbers came back online — was a reminder that he alone had survived.

The greenhouse tube saved him. By some cosmic irony, hiding away in the Luna pod he had built for privacy had spared his life. Now, Mars itself had become his Luna: endless, empty, and achingly quiet.

But Aries didn't stop. He couldn't. The first days were the worst. He worked with shaking hands, forming a permanent patch for the software glitch that had turned the CO_2 scrubbers into silent killers. He rerouted power, restored alarms, and double-wrapped every line with redundancy. He spoke out loud the entire time, partly to stay focused, partly not to feel so alone.

The worst part was removing the bodies. They would not decompose in the oxygen free environment, but they would freeze. There was a system for this. A system no one wanted to talk about, but simply it shook frozen bodies to dust.

When the Habitat was stable again, Aries stared at the now empty bunks. He refused to linger. Work was the only thing that dulled the gnawing pain. So he worked.

He connected the Greenhouse Quarter directly to Habitat Ring B, building a stable O_2 loop that could sustain him indefinitely. He reinforced the connectors with carbon-titanium supports, his small hands blackened from sealant, his hair perpetually full of dust.

From there, he turned outward.

The old exploration rovers, half-buried in sand, abandoned after test missions years ago, became his new project. He spent weeks scavenging parts, hauling cracked solar panels across ridges, cursing when bolts seized from rust. Piece by piece, he refitted them.

When the first drone hummed to life, he grinned for the first time in months.

"Rocky," he named it, after the stubborn way it trundled over jagged terrain.

The second, smaller but faster, he called "Dusty."

Together, Rocky and Dusty became his companions. Rocky hauled payloads and did heavy lifting, while Dusty zipped ahead to scout terrain. Aries programmed them with playful quirks; Rocky whistled old Earth songs as it moved; Dusty clicked like an impatient bird. The silence of Mars broke just a little.

Aries didn't survive on Mars alone. Not really. He survived because he built himself a family out of what he had left. Rocky became like a big brother. Slow, stubborn, reliable. The drone wasn't sleek; it was built from the heavy-lift rover parts Aries had scavenged, retrofitted with an exo-shell of dented alloy plating. Rocky couldn't move fast, but once it got going, nothing stopped it. Aries learned to lean on that reliability.

"Rocky, haul this crate," Aries muttered one day,

strapping nutrient tanks to its back. Rocky groaned, servos grinding, but it moved with patient inevitability. Aries grinned. "See? You're the only one around here I can count on not to complain."

The machine beeped once in what Aries swore sounded like smug agreement.

Dusty, by contrast, was the little sibling. Aries had gutted a smaller rover, reprogrammed its flight unit, and mounted twin camera stalks that gave it the eerie look of oversized eyes.

Food, power, water, climate control, everything the colony needed, Aries rebuilt with precision. The solar arrays gleamed like silver wings under the pink sky. The water reclamation system sang its soft gurgling music again. The grow lamps in the greenhouse spilled artificial daylight over rows of budding spinach, potatoes, and strawberries.

By month four, the systems purred better than when thirty trained adults had maintained them. And all of it was run by one boy who refused to quit.

But when the work stopped, loneliness pressed in. That's when Aries turned back to her.

His mother's hologram now lived in the mainframe. She wasn't just confined to the Luna pod anymore; he had expanded her code, letting her project anywhere in the colony. She flickered into existence in the galley, soft light glowing on the side of the table where she had sat during family dinners on Earth. She hummed lullabies in the greenhouse while he tended plants. She whispered encouragement when his hands shook after reprogramming an airlock.

"You're not alone, Aries," she told him, her eyes kind and endless.

"Feels like I am," he whispered.

Her hand reached out, glowing but untouchable. "Then you're stronger than you know."

And there was Skye.

Every night, Aries powered up the comm system, the delay stretching across millions of kilometers. She was still on Earth, training; her wave was not scheduled until later. Her face would flicker on screen, warm and bright, her laugh cutting through the cold metal walls. She teased him about his unkempt hair, scolded him for working nonstop, and listened when he confessed how the silence clawed at him.

"You're not just surviving," she told him once.

"You're building something. You're proving Mars can be home."

He wanted to believe her. He wanted to believe that when she arrived, she'd see more than a boy who was carrying a ghost on his back.

Six months passed. The loneliness dulled, though it never left. Mars became a routine: wake, check systems, tend crops, recalibrate drones, log progress, keep the hour, dinner at 6:00pm, talk to Skye, talk to Mom, sleep. The pattern kept him sane.

Then came the message: SECOND WAVE ARRIVAL: 142 SOLS.

Aries stared at the blinking alert until his hands trembled. People were coming. He wouldn't be alone forever. The silence would end.

But as the wind rattled the habitat walls and Rocky whistled an off-key tune in the background, Aries realized something else.

When they came, they wouldn't just see Mars. They would see what he had built.

A boy who had kept a world alive.

And for the first time since the night his mother hadn't come home, Aries allowed himself to believe in tomorrow.

. . .

His life became a series of patterns.

It had to, because without them, the silence of Mars pressed down like a gravity stronger than any on Earth. His father had once said discipline was the difference between survival and chaos. For six months, discipline became Aries's only shield.

Mornings always began the same way.

He woke at Sol 6:00, sometimes after dreams, where his mother's voice still reached him. He pulled on his jumpsuit, ran a hand through his unruly hair, and checked the Habitat Systems Console before he even brushed his teeth.

O_2: Stable.

Pressure: Normal.

Heat: Steady.

CO_2 Scrubbers: Green.

Only then did he breathe a little easier.

Breakfast was freeze-dried eggs, reconstituted spinach, or sometimes strawberries fresh from the greenhouse. He'd sit alone at the long galley table built for thirty, one boy eating in silence while the hum of the air circulators filled the space where voices used to be.

"Good morning, Aries," his mother's hologram said, flickering softly to life across the table. Her image wavered, but her smile was steady.

He half-smiled back. "Morning, Mom. Guess what? The menu's the same as always."

"Then you should be thankful," she teased. "You used to hate spinach."

He ate, not for flavor, but because Mars demanded fuel. Midday meant work. Always work.

Rocky the drone lumbered beside him, servos whining, as Aries hauled solar panels across the dusty plateau to realign them toward the weak sun. Dusty zipped overhead, scanning for stress fractures in Habitat Ring C. Aries had programmed Dusty with an attitude, quick bursts of beeps that almost sounded impatient when Aries was too slow.

"Yeah, yeah, I'm coming," he muttered, sweat stinging his eyes as the Martian sky stretched pale orange above him.

Sometimes he'd stop working and just... look.

The horizon was endless, dunes painted gold and crimson. The mountains rose like jagged teeth against a salmon-colored sky. Sunsets lingered forever, violet bleeding into ink-black, stars spilling out sharper than any seen from Earth. The beauty was breathtaking.

Because every time the stars came out, Aries wondered if his mom was among them.

By afternoon, he shifted to the greenhouse. The

steady glow of grow lamps bathed his skin in artificial sunlight. He pruned spinach, monitored root chambers, and whispered to the plants like they were teammates.

"C'mon, you're my oxygen generators," he told them. "Don't give up on me."

Mom's hologram appeared sometimes here, her voice wrapping around him like it used to at bedtime. "You're doing beautifully, Aries. She would be so proud."

He always looked away at that. "Don't," he whispered. "Not today."

Evenings were for messages.

The delay meant conversations with Skye were always fractured. She would ask a question, and twenty minutes later he could answer. Yet somehow, it worked.

Her face would light up his comm screen, cheeks smudged with grease, hair tied back in a messy bun. "Still fixing everyone's junk down here," she'd say with a grin. "You wouldn't believe how many cadets think rebooting is a 'miracle repair.'"

Aries smirked, tired but grateful. "They should

send you here. Half of these systems are stubborn as hell."

"Don't tempt me," she'd fire back. Then, softer: "Are you... okay?"

He never answered directly. Sometimes he'd change the subject, showing her Dusty's new camera upgrade or Rocky's clumsy attempts at lifting crates. Other times, when the loneliness bit deep, he'd just stare at her frozen image after transmission ended, whispering to a face that couldn't hear: "No. I'm not okay."

Nights were the hardest.

He'd retreat to the Luna pod in the greenhouse. The small privacy chamber made him feel like he was less alone. There, he'd lie back and let his mother's AI flicker to life beside him. She was more advanced now, her voice softer, her expressions more real.

"Tell me what you're thinking," she said one night, when his eyes were glassy.

"I think I killed you," he blurted.

She tilted her head, calm. "Aries..."

"You only went out because of me. Because I was sick. If I hadn't..." His throat locked. Tears blurred his vision. "You'd still be here. Dad wouldn't have left me alone. I wouldn't..."

His voice broke, the words dissolving into a sob that ripped out of him raw and unstoppable. He curled on the floor of the pod, arms tight around his chest. The AI couldn't hold him, couldn't wipe the tears, but it stayed. It stayed, and it spoke the way his real mother would have.

"You didn't take me from this world, Aries. Love did. Love is why I left that night. And love is why you're still here, fighting."

He cried until exhaustion pulled him under. He woke hours later, cheek pressed to the metal floor, eyes swollen, the pod's hum surrounding him like a lullaby. Aries loved his dad, but after he died fulfilling his dream, it was his mother he still needed.

And then, because Mars didn't pause for grief, he stood up. He worked. He lived.

SOL 142 FINALLY BROUGHT THE message: SECOND WAVE ARRIVAL.

Aries sat in the greenhouse, strawberry juice staining his fingers, Rocky humming an old Earth tune nearby. Dusty clicked overhead impatiently. Mom's hologram appeared at his side, a smile warm as sunrise.

"They're coming," she said.

"Yeah," Aries whispered. "They're coming."

He wasn't sure whether he was ready. But for the first time since the colony had gone silent, he wasn't afraid of tomorrow.

DUSTY WAS TWITCHY, restless, always circling overhead or zipping in front of him like a kid showing off.

When Aries bent over the wiring, Dusty darted in with a flash of light.

"Stop scanning me," Aries laughed, swatting at it.

"You're worse than a mosquito."

Dusty chirped a high-pitched trill and zipped away.

Still, Dusty was the one to spot cracks in solar panels or wear on oxygen seals. Annoying, but sharp. Aries began talking to it like a pesky little brother: irritated one minute, grateful the next.

His mom's AI, she was the anchor. More than the others, she felt real. In the Luna pod or the greenhouse, her hologram became the quiet listener, the patient comforter. She reminded him to eat. She reminded him to rest. Sometimes she scolded him, which almost felt good, like boundaries still existed.

"You can't work twenty hours straight," she told him one evening when he tried to push through an electrical rewire.

"Can too," he muttered.

"You'll collapse, and then what? Rocky's not certified for medical care."

He barked out a tired laugh despite himself. "Fine. You win."

Aries started timing his schedule around when Skye's replies would reach him. He'd sit by the console, fingers tapping impatiently, waiting for her face to flicker onto the screen.

One evening, her message played: "You know, Aries, everyone down here talks about you like you're some kind of legend. The kid who saved the Titan-X launch, the boy who's holding Mars by himself. But when I see you..." she leaned closer to the camera, voice softening, "... I don't see a legend. I see a boy who needs someone to remind him to laugh."

Aries stared at the frozen screen long after the transmission ended, his throat tight.

Together, they became a household.

Rocky carried the weight.

Dusty teased and nagged.

Mom soothed and advised.

Skye made him laugh and reminded him that Earth was still watching.

Aries realized he was talking to himself at dinner one night, just him at the long table, a tray of greenhouse spinach and rehydrated stew. Rocky's frame sat humming in the corner, Dusty hovered above, his mom's hologram shimmered at the seat beside him, and Skye's latest message was queued on the screen. He raised his cup of recycled water. "To family," he whispered. The silence of Mars answered back, but it didn't feel so empty.

11

SECOND WAVE

The arrival of the second wave was supposed to feel like salvation. Thirty new crew, supplies, reinforcements, proof that Earth hadn't forgotten him. But to Aries, it felt like an invasion.

Commander Roland Veyra wasted no time in establishing his rule. He was the kind of man who believed order was the same thing as oxygen; without it, you died.

The morning after his arrival, he gathered everyone in the ready room. His voice was sharp and deliberate, like every syllable had been drilled into him back on Earth.

"Effective immediately," Veyra announced, "this colony will operate under baseline Earth specifications. I want all systems returned to default configurations. The greenhouse will be isolated again, as per protocol. The rover modifications will be stripped. And the mainframe will be restored to factory code."

A murmur rippled through the crew. Aries felt his stomach drop. He didn't even wait for Veyra to finish.

"You can't do that," Aries said, standing up so fast his chair scraped against the deck. "The default systems don't work here. They didn't account for Mars's power fluctuations, or the condensation loads, or..."

"Sit down, Cadet," Veyra snapped.

Aries's fists tightened. "I saved this colony with those changes. If I hadn't patched the scrubbers, you'd all be choking in your bunks right now."

Veyra's jaw flexed, but his tone stayed cold. "You kept a malfunctioning system limping along with improvised code. That is not engineering. That is recklessness. And it ends today."

The purge began that afternoon.

Aries watched helplessly as the tech teams followed Veyra's orders. The power conduits he'd rerouted were unplugged and reconnected to the original grid. The greenhouse umbilical — the lifeline of extra O_2 and humidity — was physically decoupled from the habitat with the groan of releasing seals. Rocky and Dusty were forced offline until their Earth-approved firmware could be reinstalled.

And then came the mainframe.

Aries was on the control deck when Veyra gave the order. "Restore the system image. Wipe all unauthorized files. That includes the Karalis custom directories."

"No!" Aries said, louder than he meant. He took a step forward. "Those directories are my mother."

The room froze. A few heads turned. Veyra didn't blink.

"Whatever sentimental constructs you've been playing with," the commander said, "they're unauthorized. They interfere with mission control's ability to monitor. They go."

Aries's voice cracked. "She's not interfering. She's *her*. She's the only..." He swallowed hard. "She's the only thing I have left."

Veyra's expression hardened. "And what you have left is irrelevant to the mission." He turned to the systems officer. "Proceed."

The officer hesitated, glancing at Aries. His

cursor hovered. Aries lunged forward, shoving at the officer. "Don't you dare!"

Two engineers stepped in, catching him under the arms, dragging him back. Aries kicked, shouted, but the screen lit with the progress bar all the same:

Mainframe Restore — 8%... 22%... 41%

"Stop it!" Aries screamed, throat raw. "You don't understand; she helped me survive! She kept me sane when I was *alone*!"

Veyra stood over him, arms crossed, voice unyielding. "Enough. This is not about you. This is about Mars. And Mars is bigger than your grief."

The bar hit **100%**. The screen went black. And when it came back, the directories were gone.

Aries went still. The fight drained out of his body all at once. His chest felt hollow, as if the oxygen had been ripped from the room. He whispered so low that only the engineer holding his shoulder could hear:

"You just killed her again."

That night, Aries didn't return to his bunk. He couldn't. He could not bring himself to be anywhere near that cold-blooded murderer. Instead, he slipped into the greenhouse under cover of dark. Luna still lived there, hidden deep in the isolated tube he had built, her code running on a private loop the purge couldn't touch.

Aries took a moment to enable his drones. Rocky and Dusty were his loyal family, and he needed them.

He crawled inside and pressed his forehead to the cool glass of the interface. "They don't want you here," he said hoarsely. "But I do." For the first time since the second wave arrived, he let himself cry. His mom was not the same; she had lost months of adaptation. The main chatbot survived in Luna, she had lost so much data. He needed her just the same. He explained everything that had happened. She listened more than talked, but seeing her image helped.

Aries was talking to his mom late into the night when he heard the sound of Dusty's alarm chime echoing inside Luna's tube. The tone wasn't playful like usual. It was sharp, clipped. Urgent.

He blinked the tears from his eyes. The habitat was in trouble. Dusty confirmed. The drone's voice came through the greenhouse intercom, mechanical but laced with the inflections Aries had coded into it months ago.

"Alert. Oxygen scrubbers offline. Pressure drop

detected in Habitat A. Alarm protocols... disabled."

Aries's blood went cold. His stomach turned. He lay in the tube, not moving.

"They didn't want my help." Aries exhaled, "They don't deserve my help."

"You need to help them." His mom advised him.

Aries sulked, not wanting to accept what was the right course.

"Not because they are good, but because you are." His mother was right.

He bolted across the greenhouse, barely shoving his arms through the sleeves of his jumpsuit. His boots slipped on the condensation floor plates as he grabbed his helmet and sealed it in one practiced motion.

Rocky clattered to life near the hydroponic tanks, chirping his high-pitched warning.

"Atmosphere unstable. Crew vitals declining."

Aries froze at those words. Crew vitals. They were inside. Ten minutes away. Ten minutes too long.

His chest burned with a familiar agony, the same one from six months ago. The same one that had left him standing in a colony of corpses. It was happening again.

"They didn't listen!" Aries shouted, slamming his fist against the greenhouse hatch as it sealed behind him. His voice reverberated in his helmet, raw and furious.

He ran across the red sand, the weak Martian gravity making each stride too long, too floating, as if mocking his urgency.

Dusty rolled alongside, wheels spitting dust.

"Recommend immediate return to Habitat A. Time to depletion: 6 minutes, 41 seconds."

Aries's breath rasped in his ears. His mind raced faster than his legs. The update. Of course. The damned update had rolled back when Veyra reset the mainframe. It had cut the heaters, cut the scrubbers, silenced the alarms — the exact cascade Aries had spent weeks fixing.

He knew this would happen. He *warned* them.

Now again they would die refusing to trust him.

By the time he reached the habitat airlock, the world was too quiet. The hum of systems was gone, the comforting vibration of life support missing. Just stillness.

Aries keyed the override, his gloves slipping on the panel as his hands shook. The inner door opened, and the sight that met him hollowed his chest.

They were all there.

Commander Veyra slumped against the wall, his face frozen in a half-snarl. The systems officers sprawled near their stations. Thirty people in silence, bodies slack, lips tinged blue.

Peaceful. Exactly like before.

Aries staggered into the room, helmet still sealed, oxygen hissing into his own private bubble. His pulse hammered in his ears, but the rest of the habitat was lifeless.

For a long moment, he just stood there, shaking. His anger, his grief, his guilt — all tangled into one unbearable knot. He wanted to scream. He wanted to smash Veyra's frozen face. He wanted to cry into his mother's AI until the pain bled out of him.

But he forced himself to move.

He tore open the system panel, yanked the access port, and keyed in his old patches from memory. His fingers flew across the holographic keys, muscle memory overriding the tremor of his rage.

"Manual patch initiated. CO_2 scrubbers: reboot. Heater relays: bypass. Alarm grid: restore."

The hum of life-support systems roared back to life, too late to save anyone but him.

Aries slumped against the console, panting, helmet still on. His reflection stared back at him from the blank monitor — a boy alone, sealed in glass, in a colony built on death.

He whispered hoarsely, voice cracking through the helmet's comm pickup: "I told you. I told you this would happen."

Dusty's lens blinked blue beside him. Rocky chirped low and mournfully. But there was no answer from anyone else. Just like before, Aries Karalis was alone on Mars.

12

THE FALLOUT

The comms room felt cavernous in its silence. The walls hummed faintly with redirected power from the greenhouse; Aries's modifications had seen to that, but there were no voices, no shuffling bodies, no routine banter before a log. Only him.

Aries slid into the command chair and keyed in the long-range uplink. The screen flickered with static, then steadied into the emblem of the **Mars Expedition Corp**. After a pause, a woman's face appeared, washed in the pale blue glow of Earth-side servers. She wore a crisp suit of a perfect assistant, expression carefully neutral.

"Mars Colony, Wave Two, status report received. Please confirm your…"

Aries leaned forward, slamming the transmit key. "They're all dead."

The woman blinked, lips parting in surprise. "Aries... clarify."

"You heard me!" he snapped. His voice was raw, the kind of rasp that came from too much screaming into an empty room. "Every single one of them. Veyra, the systems officers, the whole damn crew. They're gone."

The woman's practiced calm wavered. "We... we show no distress signals, no critical faults. Are you certain about the colony..."

Aries slammed his fist against the console, the sound reverberating through the link.

"Of course I'm certain! I'm the one dragging their bodies out of the habitat!" His throat tightened, but the anger burned hotter than the grief.

"Do you know why they're dead? Because you, all of you, back on your safe little blue marble, thought your protocols meant more than survival.

You reset the systems. You deleted my fixes. You stripped out the patches that kept us alive!"

The woman faltered. Behind her, blurred figures shifted, supervisors listening in. A man's voice broke through: "Aries, slow down. The second-wave commander was under direct orders to restore base-line operating standards. Deviations compromise..."

"Compromise survival? Is that what you were going to say?" Aries shouted, cutting him off. His face filled the monitor, pale with exhaustion and rage. "You think your paperwork knows Mars better than I do? You think some policy drafted on Earth is worth more than the air we breathe here? I warned Veyra. I begged him not to reset the mainframe. And now thirty more are dead because you wanted things neat and tidy in your manuals."

The silence on the other end was suffocating.

Aries leaned back, chest heaving. His eyes glistened, but his jaw was set like stone.

"This is on you. You didn't lose just a crew. You lost trust. You lost the colony. From now on, Mars runs on my terms, or it doesn't run at all."

"Aries..." the woman began, voice softer now.

He cut the feed. The screen went black. For a long moment, Aries just sat there, breathing hard in the darkened comm room. His reflection hovered in the dead glass: a boy with too many ghosts, too much anger, and nowhere left to put it.

Behind him, Dusty rolled forward and spoke in his clipped, mechanical voice: **"Transmission** complete. Emotional intensity: high. Recommend a rest cycle."

Aries gave a short, bitter laugh. "Yeah," he whispered. "Rest. Like that's possible."

Then he stood, turned his back on the empty screen, and walked out into the colony he now commanded alone, again.

THE GLASS-WALLED CONFERENCE room at Mission Control Arizona was sealed tight, but the arguments inside still seemed to rattle the structure.

Director Erick Caulder sat at the head of the long table, hands steepled beneath his chin, the faint glow of a dozen screens reflecting in his tired eyes. The footage of Aries's transmission, his furious, grief-wracked condemnation, had already played twice. No one needed a third. The silence after it ended had been louder than the boy's voice.

Finally, Captain Richter of the Wave Three security team broke the quiet.

"He's a liability. A kid, no matter how smart. You can't let a fifteen-year-old dictate survival strategies on Mars."

"A fifteen-year-old who's still alive," muttered Dr. Maris Klien, the systems biologist. She shoved her glasses higher on her nose and jabbed at her data pad. "We've buried fifty-nine qualified adults. Two full waves gone. And the one who outlived them all is the kid who rewrote the systems to actually work."

"Because he cheated," Richter snapped. "He rewrote protocols. He introduced unauthorized code into our network. That alone..."

"... Saved his life," Klien cut in, sharp as a scalpel. "And could've saved everyone else's if Commander Veyra had listened."

At the far end, Commander Halima Ortiz tapped her fingers against the table. She had been chosen to lead Wave Three, her reputation built on unbending discipline. Her voice was calm, but hard as steel.

"We cannot build a colony based on improvisation. Order must be maintained. Procedures exist because they're tested. If every cadet starts rewriting the handbook..."

"Aries isn't every cadet," said Dr. Laney Sierra, head of psychological operations. Her tone was weary, but fierce. "He's a prodigy with a survival record no one else has matched. He's resourceful, adaptable, and he has the trust of the environment we're sending people into. Like it or not, he is the handbook on Mars right now."

The table broke into crosstalk. Words like chain

of command, maverick, catastrophic oversight, and public fallout collided until Caulder raised his hand. The room hushed.

He leaned forward, his voice low, deliberate.

"The loss of Waves One and Two is already history's loudest failure. Billions of dollars. Decades of preparation. And nearly sixty souls in Martian soil. We can't afford a third failure. Not politically. Not financially. Not morally."

He glanced at the frozen frame of Aries on the central display, the boy's eyes blazing, his knuckles white against the console.

"The fact is," Caulder continued, "Aries Karalis has kept himself alive for over a year in the harshest conditions imaginable. He's not just surviving. He's building. He's developed drone infrastructure, greenhouse integration, and climate stabilization. None of that was in the playbook. But it works."

Richter scowled. "So we just let him play President of Mars?"

"No," Caulder said firmly. He looked around the table, voice steady, brooking no argument. "We listen to him. We defer to his expertise on Martian conditions because he's the only one with real experience. But every decision, every modification, every deviation from Earth-standard protocol will be reported back here. We decide what stands. He's our man on the ground. We're still the command in the sky."

Commander Ortiz frowned but inclined her head. Klien exhaled in relief. Richter offered the faintest of nods.

Caulder rapped his knuckles once against the table. "That's the directive. Aries consults on Mars. But the chain of command still ends here. If he's the spark keeping our dream alive, we will be the ones shaping the flame."

The meeting broke into murmurs again, softer now, but no less tense. On the screen, Aries's frozen image seemed to glare down at them all — a boy caught between genius and grief, the ghost of two dead waves pressing on his shoulders.

For the first time, Director Caulder wondered if Mars's survival depended not on the people they sent, but on whether one stubborn, brilliant teenager could bear the weight of being right.

ARIES WAS HALFWAY through logging the last oxygen cycle when Dusty trilled from the airlock. **"Movement detected. Rover Two. Heat signature present."**

Aries's stomach dropped. For a heartbeat, he

thought it was a ghost, his mind playing tricks. Everyone else was gone. He had checked. He had seen them all. But the rover's monitor lit up with a faint, steady pulse of heat. Someone *alive*.

Aries sprinted across the red sands, Rocky bumping along behind him like a loyal dog. The rover sat buried in dust outside the southern bay, its exterior coated in a thin crust of frost. Aries scrambled up the side ladder and pounded his gloved fist against the sealed hatch.

"Hello?!" His voice cracked inside the helmet. "If you can hear me, wake up!"

No answer. He banged harder, nearly frantic. Through the small viewport, he spotted movement: a man slumped in the pilot's chair, head tilted back, a bottle glinting in one hand. Scotch.

"Are you kidding me?" Aries muttered. "You drunken idiot."

He slammed his palm against the hatch again. "HEY! Wake up! Get your helmet on, or you're dead the second I open this!"

Inside, the man stirred, groaning. He blinked blearily, his beard ragged, his eyes bloodshot. Aries could just make out the words he mouthed: *The hell...?*

"Helmet!" Aries shouted, jabbing a finger at his own. "Put it on, now!"

Slowly, grumbling, the man fumbled under the seat and dragged out his helmet, slapping it into place with sluggish hands. He gave Aries a thumbs-up that was more like a middle finger, then reached for the hatch controls.

The door hissed open, cold air rushing in past Aries's boots. The man stumbled out, bottle still in his grip, and staggered onto the sand.

Aries grabbed his arm to steady him. "You almost died. Do you know that?"

The man gave a raspy laugh. His voice was deep, gravelly, with a hint of an old Southern drawl. "Kid, I've almost died more times than I can count. Rover was warmer than the bunks, and hell, I wasn't about to share my scotch with others."

Aries glared up at him. "Scotch just saved your life."

The man barked a laugh, coughed, then shook his head. "You're funny. I like that. Major Carl Atlas at your service. And you are?"

"Aries Karalis," he said, still bristling. "And I'm the one who just saved your sorry life."

Carl smirked. "Thanks." He tilted the bottle, offering. "Want a drink? You've earned it."

Aries pushed it away. "I don't drink. And if you plan to stay alive here, maybe you shouldn't either."

Carl studied him for a long moment, the smile fading. "You did just say it saved my life." He tucked the bottle into a pocket. "You're the smart one, huh? The genius kid who kept this place running."

Aries stiffened. "I did, but they didn't listen. They reset everything, and now they're..." His voice cracked. He swallowed hard. "Now they're gone."

Carl's expression appeared puzzled. He clapped a heavy hand on Aries's shoulder. "What do you mean, gone?"

Aries blinked. For the first time, the man's eyes looked less bloodshot, more tired. "Come on, it's probably better that you see for yourself."

They walked back to the habitat together in silence, their boots crunching over red gravel. Inside, Aries reconnected the scrubbers while Carl slumped into a chair, blinking his eyes and shaking his head as if that would wake him from a dream where the others were dead.

Finally, Carl spoke. "Kid. I've been through hell-holes before. War zones. Jungles. Places where everyone dies, but me. And you know what I learned?" He leaned forward, fixing Aries with a steady veteran's stare. "Nobody survives alone. Not for long. You need someone watching your six. Someone who knows how to fight, how to keep the wolves from the door."

Aries folded his arms. "And you think that's you."

Carl stared steadily and coldly. "Damn right. You're the brains, kid. Smarter than anyone I've met. But brains don't mean much if you get blindsided. You and I, we cover each other; you keep Mars from killing me, and I'll make sure they listen to you."

Aries hesitated. He thought of his mother's AI, of Dusty and Rocky, of Skye on Earth. And then of the twenty-nine silent bodies in the habitat.

Slowly, he extended his hand. "Deal."

Carl gripped it, firm and calloused. "Good. Then we survive on this rock together. Mars just got itself one hell of a team."

For the first time since losing his father, Aries felt something loosen in his chest. Maybe, just maybe, he wasn't alone anymore.

13

THE NEXT CORRECT THING

The Titan-12 rose from Earth in a tower of white fire, splitting the morning clouds as if tearing the sky in half. From Mars, the launch feed arrived minutes old, but Aries still leaned into the flickering screen as if time itself might shorten if he willed it.

The roar rattled the speakers, tinny and distant, but enough to bring a lump to his throat. Flames licked the booster stages, smoke coiling down across a coastline, he could barely remember the smell of — salt and wet sand, the kind of things Mars had stripped from his life.

And then, Skye. The camera caught her just before she stepped through the hatch, cadet cap tugged low, hair tucked tight. She winked straight into the lens, lips moving in words Aries knew were meant for him.

"See you soon, Mars."

He replayed it three times, then shut the feed off before Atlas caught him staring. Atlas gave Aries a knowing nod, but didn't say anything.

Six months out, Titan-12 was already a world of its own. The ready room was full of drifting bodies, magnetic boots clinking softly as they anchored to the deck. The air was metallic, scrubbed thin and humming with fans. Commander Halima Ortiz floated at the front like she'd been carved from iron. Her cropped hair framed a face that betrayed nothing.

"We're not passengers," she told them, voice low but sharp enough to cut through the stale air. "We arrive as a unit. Disciplined. Prepared. Mars is unforgiving. Protocol will guide us. Adaptation will save us."

Her words hung in the recycled air.

Dr. Marissa Klein, medical, pinched the bridge of her nose, muttering, "As a whole, the crew wasn't drinking enough water."

Commander Ortiz noted, "I imagined it was nervousness; continue to monitor."

Nevin Carter, power officer, had his tablet

already pulled apart into diagnostics, lips pressed thin, brain clearly four moves ahead, "all systems nominal."

Jamie Acosta, agriculture officer, laughed under her breath, the sound like sunlight breaking through. "I'm excited to see the greenhouse. Reports are spotty, but the trees should be producing if they are still alive." She flashed her brilliant smile.

Otto Schmidt, structural officer, grunted in reply, his deep voice vibrating in the panels. "Minimal change during launch should mean an uneventful voyage."

Commander nodded. "Uneventful sounds good to me."

Andrew Hess, comms officer, said nothing, just adjusted his headset and watched. Always watching.

Diego Ramos, life support, paced even in zero-g, boots scraping, muttering about decimals in oxygen ratios.

Samuel Cambell, habitat, didn't look up from his notes. "Numbers don't lie. People do. Trust the systems."

"Settle in folks, from here, there is a lot of waiting. In six months, we will have to be on our A-game; for now, get some rest." Commander Ortiz stated.

At the back, three security officers clung to the

wall like shadows, eyes flat, silent as stone. They basically had no responsibility until they reached Mars, so kept themselves entertained with dares and challenges.

And there was Skye Enyo, stylus behind her ear, smirk curling her lip. She leaned to a cadet and whispered, "Let's just hope Mars doesn't get us, as it got the other waves. I hope they will listen to Aries. If so, we may have a chance."

The Cadet gave a nervous laugh that bubbled quickly. Ortiz's gaze flicked over, sharp as a blade, but she said nothing.

On Mars, Aries and Atlas worked beneath the rust-colored sky. The wind outside sang against the domes, a low moaning whistle that never stopped. Inside, the habitat hummed with the life they had forced into being.

The greenhouse and habitat were joined forever now. They could walk from the habitat to the green-house through a corridor. Instead of taking twenty minutes, it took two. Carbon, oxygen, water, all cycled in harmony. The faint scent of soil, real soil, rich and dark, hung in the air.

Power grids glowed blue on the monitors, triple-layered, every line cross-checked. Titan-X and II rockets had been gutted, their fuel cells retooled into backup reserves. Atlas ran his scarred hand over the panel, rough against smooth alloy, and grunted with satisfaction.

"Kid," he said, voice low as gravel, "if this system fails, it means the damn sun has quit shining."

Aries almost smiled.

The trees had taken hold in the greenhouse dome, slender trunks stretching up, leaves trembling beneath grow lights. Apples, citrus, figs and stone fruits. Their scent was faint but unmistakable, a ghost of Earth. The first apple he bit was sharp, tart juice exploding across his tongue. His chest ached at the memory it unlocked. Aries saved the seeds and started new saplings. He dreamed of entire orchards thriving on the red planet.

"Mom, you'd love this," he whispered.

Eleni's voice, soft as a lullaby, replied, "You did the next correct thing, Aries."

She was now fully integrated in the mainframe. Her hologram could follow him throughout the colony.

"Mom, will you extend the daylight cycle by thirty minutes?" Aries asked.

"Done," she replied.

They had not forgotten the dead. The frozen bodies were put through the shaker. Wave One and

Two had been returned to the soil with as much reverence as could be spared. The compost enriched the greenhouse beds, their names etched on the walls of the greenhouse. The wall was a monument to the sacrifice and elements, given to keep the colony growing. Aries traced a finger across one, his throat closing.

Atlas set his palm on another and muttered, "They deserved better than the damned Veyra. I never could stand a commander who followed blindly."

The silence between them said the rest.

The mainframe was no longer vulnerable. Aries had learned his lesson. He had locked it with encryption so dense it would take years to crack, layered with a physical cage that required both his and Atlas's hands.

"No one wipes Mom again," he muttered.

Atlas clapped him on the shoulder, rough and steady. "Over my dead body, kid."

Aries appreciated having Atlas at his side. A kid could be dismissed easily; Atlas never did that, never even thought to try to take charge.

His father had left him with the philosophy, "the next correct thing." It had stuck with him. At first,

Atlas had mocked it, rolling his eyes. But now he spoke it like gospel.

"You know," Atlas said one night, tearing open a protein bar, "I used to live ten steps ahead. Always planning for the worst. This... this thing your dad said? Works better than a map. Clears the noise. Keeps me standing."

Aries looked at him, a faint smile ghosting across his lips. "That's Dad."

The comms console blinked with Skye's latest message. Aries leaned forward, heart kicking faster.

Skye: *They bunked me with the greenhouse cadets. Guess I'll have to prove I can grow more than bean sprouts.*

Aries: *Beans keep you alive. Don't knock them.*

Skye: *Fine, bean boy. You better save me an apple.*

Aries: *I'll trade you an apple for a kiss.*

Skye: *Cheeky. Save both.*

Atlas caught him grinning at the screen, cheeks flushed. He barked a laugh that rattled the tools on the workbench.

"Oh, this is rich. Mars's boy genius can rebuild oxygen scrubbers in his sleep but loses his head over a girl."

Aries hurled a spanner at him, face burning.

Atlas had a big, stupid grin on his face. "Touched a nerve there, didn't I?"

EVERY NIGHT, Aries crawled into the command bunk, closed his eyes, and spoke to his mother. He told her about the apple trees, about Atlas, about Skye. The hum of air recyclers filled the silence between her words, the gentle white noise of survival.

"You've done more than survive, Aries," his mom told him one night. "You've built life. Don't forget to live in it." He curled tighter in the bunk, breathing her voice like oxygen.

SIX MONTHS BECAME ROUTINE. Repairs, drills, Atlas's rough jokes, Mom's soft reminders, Skye's teasing notes. The rhythm of survival became the rhythm of living. Rocky and Dusty continued to be invaluable. Rocky made building new infrastructure possible. Dusty facilitated scouting and delivery of small tools.

Then, one pale Martian dawn, Aries stepped into the greenhouse walkway and froze. A glint cut the sky, silver and sharp as a blade. Titan-12, burn after burn, was coming down.

Wave Three was here.

And with them, Skye Enyo.

14

RED CARPET

The Titan-12 came down slowly, thrusters kicking up a storm of red dust that rolled across the landing pad like a curtain. Aries squinted through his visor as Atlas's hand clamped down on his shoulder, steadying him against the vibration that thudded through the ground.

"Textbook," Atlas muttered. His voice was low, gravelly, but even he couldn't hide the edge of relief.

The descent burn cut off. Silence. Then the hiss and clang of landing struts biting into Martian bedrock.

A hatch opened, and the first boots of Wave Three touched down. Their suits gleamed new and bright, still smelling clean after 6 months in a sterile environment. Aries's own suit bore scratches, patches, smears of regolith dust ground into the joints. He wondered if they'd notice.

"Showtime," Atlas said.

Rocky trundled forward on thick treads, manipulators already reaching for the cargo crates being lowered by the crew. The machine's sensors blinked like eager eyes.

"Unit...uh, designation?" one officer asked, startled.

"Rocky," Aries said, voice matter-of-fact. "He can do a lot more than help with load transfers."

Commander Halima Ortiz tilted her helmet slightly, watching the machine hoist a half-ton crate like it was nothing. Her tone was cool but not dismissive. "Impressive. Adaptive use of resources."

Atlas smirked behind his visor. "That's one way to put it."

Then she was there. Skye. She didn't walk; she half-ran across the pad, boots clanking, arms outstretched as much as the bulky suit would allow. She slammed into him, the two of them locked in an awkward embrace of helmets and hard polymer chest plates.

It didn't matter. Aries felt the thump of her against him, the warmth of her effort, the way her breath fogged her faceplate. He hugged back tight. The suit stole the softness, but the meaning was clear.

"About damn time," she said, voice crackling over the comms.

"Yeah," Aries breathed. "About time."

Inside the habitat, the questions began immediately. Too many questions. The seven systems officers spread out like bees swarming a hive, eyes darting from screen to system to joint seal. Klein tested a med scanner on herself and frowned at the calibration. Carter crouched by the new power grid, silent, stylus flicking across his pad at a furious pace. Acosta actually laughed at the sight of dwarf apple trees, reaching to touch a branch with reverence. Schmidt muttered something in German that Aries didn't need a translator for — half awe, half skepticism. Hess leaned into the comm hub, lips pressed thin. Ramos's brows crashed together the moment he saw the scrubber layout. Schmidt tapped the reinforced seal between greenhouse and habitat like he couldn't decide whether to admire it or tear it apart.

"This isn't... standard," Ramos finally said, heat rising in his voice.

"No," Aries replied, standing straighter than he

felt. "It's Mars standard. Earth systems failed. Twice. This works."

The silence that followed was thick, the officers exchanging looks.

Commander Ortiz raised a gloved hand. "We'll review systems in sequence. For now, everyone gets settled."

Housing was simple: a ring of cabins, each small but private. Aries had made sure of it. He walked Skye down the corridor, Rocky clanking behind them with her luggage perched like a prize.

"Here," Aries said, stopping at the cabin next to his. He palmed the hatch, and it slid open with a hiss. "This one's yours."

Skye blinked. "Next to you?"

"Yeah. Makes sense. You'll need quick access to systems training, and..." He hesitated. "And it's just easier."

Commander Ortiz's voice cut sharp across the hall. "Cadets do not bunk in officer quarters."

Aries turned. His chin was high, but his hands had curled into fists at his sides. "She stays here. It's how we do things."

Ortiz studied him for a long moment. Her eyes flicked from Aries to Skye to the officers now quietly unpacking down the hall. Finally, she gave the faintest nod. "Too soon to start fights," she murmured, almost to herself. Then louder: "Fine. But the rules will be addressed in time."

Aries didn't answer. He opened the door wider, letting Skye step inside.

At dinner, Aries insisted on tradition. "Six sharp," he told them, standing in the middle of the habitat commons. "Everyone. No exceptions. We eat together."

Several officers looked up, surprised at the authority in his voice. Atlas stood at the edge of the room, arms folded, not saying a word, but the ghost of a smile tugged at his scarred face.

Later, in his cabin, Aries stared at his reflection in the small metal mirror. His dress coat was too short at the wrists, the fabric pulling when he raised his arms. He swallowed. His father's coat — stiff, dark, worn from command. It smelled faintly of dust and recycled air, the scent that clung to everything on Mars.

THE HABITAT'S mess hall was narrow but long, a row of steel warmed by low amber lights. The tables stretched nearly the length of the room, brushed aluminum polished by years of use.

Aries had set it himself, utensils aligned with care, ration packs heated and arranged like a feast. He wanted this to matter. To feel human.

At six sharp, the officers filed in, still in their crisp uniforms. They looked stiff, uncomfortable in the thin Martian air. Atlas came last, broad shoulders filling the doorway, eyes flicking across the room like he was still on patrol.

Aries took the commander's seat at the head of the table. He hesitated, almost sat elsewhere, but Atlas's firm hand pressed his shoulder down. "Stay."

Skye slid into the chair at his right, a quick grin flashing before she composed herself. Atlas sat at his left, arms crossed, daring anyone to object.

The others filled in, boots scraping against the deck, voices low.

"Meal looks better than the freeze-dried sludge we trained on," Jamie Acosta said, breaking the silence. She picked up a slice of roasted root vegetable, inspecting it like treasure. "You grew this here?"

"In the greenhouse," Aries said. "The crops matured faster once we rebalanced the light cycle, and the high CO_2 works miracles."

Jamie laughed, the sound bright in the close air.

"Mars-grown food with actual flavor. Bless you, Karalis."

Otto Schmidt snorted. "Food's one thing. But these systems..." He stabbed his fork toward the habitat bulkhead. "Not by the book. None of it. The mainframe feels... alien."

"It's not alien," Aries shot back. "It's Martian. Earth's systems don't work here. What you trained on would have killed you, like it nearly killed me."

Dr. Klein leaned forward, eyes sharp. "Explain."

Aries took a breath. He glanced once at Atlas, who gave a subtle nod. Then he launched in, words pouring fast, precise, his voice carrying down the table.

"The scrubbers glitched after the last software update. The heaters shut down. The O2 alarms went silent. Everyone in the habitat suffocated while they slept. Wave One. Wave Two. Gone. The only reason I'm still alive is that I was in the greenhouse that night. I patched the update and locked the systems. Now everything's redundant, shielded, and tied into the greenhouse cycle. If the habitat scrubs fail, the trees carry the load. If power grids collapse, rover cells take over. Nothing runs without dual fail-safes. It works because it has to. On Earth, a failure is an inconvenience; here, it's death."

The table went quiet except for the hum of the circulation fans. Even Ramos, who had looked ready to argue, shut his mouth.

Commander Ortiz finally leaned forward, eyes fixed on Aries. "I appreciate what you've accomplished, Cadet Karalis. But you are not the commander of this colony. That role falls to me, by order of Earth command. Protocols exist for a reason. I expect the colony to follow them."

Aries froze. His fork hovered over his plate. His chest felt tight. He was still a cadet, wasn't he? Still too young, too raw, too tied to mistakes he couldn't undo. He opened his mouth, but nothing came.

Atlas's hand came down heavy on the table. The clang silenced every voice.

"Wrong," Atlas said, voice like stone grinding against stone. His eyes locked on Ortiz. "Karalis is the Base Commander. He was field promoted. Only surviving members of Waves One and Two. He kept this place alive when Earth's pretty rulebook got everyone else killed. That coat he's wearing? He earned it. More than anyone in this room."

The officers shifted uneasily. Klein's brow furrowed. Hess's pen stopped mid-scratch. Ramos muttered something under his breath, quickly silenced by Hess's sharp elbow.

Ortiz's jaw tightened. She studied Aries again, her eyes narrowing. Testing him.

Aries swallowed hard. He wanted to shrink, to slip back into cadet skin and let someone else carry the weight. But Atlas's words pressed against him like armor, his father's coat heavy across his shoulders.

He raised his chin.

"Dinner's at six every night," he said, voice steady now. "No exceptions. We eat together. That's the rule."

Ortiz held his gaze. A muscle ticked in her cheek. Then finally she gave a small nod and leaned back.

For now, at least, Aries Karalis sat at the head of the table, shrugged into his father's coat, tugging at the sleeves until it fit as best it could. The shoulders were broad, the weight solid.

For tonight, Aries Karalis would wear his father's coat, but also fill his shoes.

THAT NIGHT AT LIGHTS OUT, Aries invited Skye to his room. "Nothing weird, I just really want to show you something."

"Seems fishy to me," Skye said as she studied his face for his intentions.

"I mean if you're scared? I get it," he said with a smirk.

"Whatever," she said, rolling her eyes.

"Nice, I like what you've done to the place."

Skye smiled at the picture on the nightstand. She picked it up, looking at his parents and him when he was younger.

"Come here, watch." He guided her to the bed.

She lay on the bunk, her back to the headboard, and he went to the other side to lie down next to her. It barely fit them both.

"Ready?" he asked.

She nodded.

"Mom."

His mother shimmered before them. "Hello Aries, Who's your friend?"

"This is Skye Enyo. I have told you about her before."

"Oh yes, hello Skye, thank you for being kind to my son. He has a very high opinion of you." Eleni said in a soft tone.

"I speak with my mom each night before bed; it has become a ritual." Aries said softly.

"Aries, Commander Ortiz is communicating with mission control on Earth. Do you want me to block the call?" his mom reported.

"No, it's fine, just alert me of anything I should be worried about," Aries said. His mom faded away.

"She really is connected to every system, isn't she?"

"Yes, she has made the entire place better." Aries explained.

"Thank you for sharing her with me; I know how much she means to you," Skye said, leaning her head on Aries shoulder.

"Do you ever worry about AI taking over? I mean it happens in the movies all the time," Skye teased.

"No, mom would never do that."

"I'm glad to be here with you. I've got your back too." Skye said.

Skye got up to head to her cabin. Aries hurried to catch up with her. He wrapped his arms her, "I'm happy you're here too."

Skye melted into him. They just held each other, enjoying the connection, listening to each other breathe. Neither wanted to be the first to break the hug. Finally, Skye said good night. Aries stepped into the hall to make sure she had everything she needed.

"Would you join me each night for my talks with my mother?" Aries asked, wondering if it sounded weird.

"I would be honored, but I don't want to intrude on your private time." Skye said.

"I would like to include you in everything." Aries admitted.

Commander Ortiz was entering her cabin at just that moment. Aries nodded to her as he returned to his cabin.

15

A NEW DAY

The colony gathered in the central commons, thirty-two souls in all, their faces lit by the UV lights and the faint glow of Martian sunrise seeping through the viewport above. Aries stood at the head of the hall, the steel edge of the table under his palms. His father's coat hung heavy across his shoulders, too big at the sleeves, but steadying him. Atlas stood off to his left like a stone wall, silent, watchful.

Aries cleared his throat. His voice cracked once, and he swallowed, forcing it steady.

"Listen up. I don't care if you're responsible for agriculture, water, or energy. Out here, those lines don't matter. We're not Earth Command's experiment. We're survivors, and survival depends on all of us. Every system, every job, every person. If you see something that doesn't work, if you have a better way, you bring it to us. We adapt, or we don't last. That's how this place runs."

A murmur swept the room, not of discontent but of energy. Faces leaned forward, heads nodding.

Dr. Marissa Klein spoke first, her clipped accent carrying clearly. "Medical autonomy, then? I see patients, I decide treatment, no waiting for Earth approval?"

"Yes," Aries said. "Your call. You're the doctor."

Klein's lips tightened, but she gave a small nod. Respect, not rebellion.

Nevin Carter, hunched over his tablet as always, spoke without looking up. "If I find efficiencies in power flow, I apply them?"

"Immediately," Aries said.

The faintest smirk crossed Schmidt's lips before he bent back to his notes.

Jamie Acosta nearly bounced in her seat. "Agriculture unrestricted? I'm free to try anything? Cross-breeding, genetic tweaking, pushing growth cycles?" Her grin was wide, almost manic with possibility.

Aries couldn't help but smile. "It's your garden, Acosta. Make it thrive."

She clapped her hands together, laughing loudly enough to fill the hall. "Finally!"

Even Schmidt cracked a grin at that, shaking his head.

But not everyone was smiling.

Commander Halima Ortiz sat stiff-backed near the end of the table, her arms crossed, jaw locked tight. Her eyes burned with disapproval. She said nothing, but her silence spoke like a hammer.

Andrew Hess, Communications, raised a hand slightly. "What about mainframe access? I can't monitor relays properly without unrestricted systems data."

Sitting beside Commander Ortiz, Diego Ramos, Life Support, nodded hard. "And I need diagnostics. Locked systems mean blind systems. That's unacceptable."

Aries met their eyes, voice firm. "The mainframe stays locked. Redundancy is manual. No remote resets. We lost two waves because of blind trust in Earth updates. That doesn't happen again. If you need data, you come to me or Atlas."

Ramos's face flushed red. Hess pressed his lips thin, bowing his head but not agreeing.

From the shadows near the bulkhead, three members of the Wave Three security detail exchanged glances, eyes flicking to Ortiz. Their loyalty was clear without a word spoken. Their purpose was not disclosed to Aries or Atlas. They watched and gathered information; they reported only to Commander Ortiz.

Aries let the silence stretch, then straightened. "This isn't about comfort. It's about survival. You want Earth's way, go back. You want to live here, really live, then this is how we do it. We listen to each other. We adapt. And we keep moving forward."

A pause. Then Acosta slapped her palm against the table. "Mars isn't Earth. I say we make it better."

Klein inclined her head, slow and deliberate. Carter muttered, "Agreed," without looking up. Even Schmidt grunted his assent.

Ortiz sat unmoving, lips pressed into an iron line.

But most of the crew leaned forward now, murmuring, nodding, a spark of excitement alive in their eyes. For the first time since landing, Aries felt the room shift, not away from him, but toward him.

Atlas caught his eye. Gave a slow, approving nod.

·   ·   ·

THE HUM of circulation fans followed them as Aries led Skye down the greenhouse corridor, the floor vibrating faintly under their boots. The colony no longer felt like a tomb; it pulsed with life, voices echoing in distant halls, machinery clicking and hissing as if the entire base was breathing.

Skye walked beside him, helmet tucked under her arm. "So this is your kingdom, huh? King of Mars giving the grand tour."

Aries snorted. "It's not a kingdom. It's a community."

"A community with strawberries," she teased, wrinkling her nose at the sweet tang of fruit in the air, as they neared the Greenhouse.

Acosta practically danced between rows of green. "Ah, finally, someone who appreciates miracles!" She pressed a strawberry into Skye's palm, then shoved another at Aries.

Skye bit into hers, eyes widening. "Oh my god. It tastes so sweet."

Aries chewed slower, letting the juice run across his tongue. He thought of his mother's garden, the way his mother used to hum while trimming basil leaves. The memory hit sharply enough to sting.

Jamie was already pulling them deeper into the greenhouse. "Wave Three brought ten thousand varieties. I can grow coffee, rice, beans, you name it. In five years, you'll eat better here than in New York."

Skye leaned closer to Aries, whispering. "She's like... glowing. I've never seen anyone so happy about dirt and leaves."

"She's not just happy," Aries murmured back. "She sees the future. She believes this place can be more than a cage."

A bee flew by, surprising Aries. "What's this?"

Jamie laughed. "We can't produce food at scale by manually pollinating."

"Does that mean..." Aries started to ask.

"Yes, we have honey." She pointed to the hives.

"You are a miracle worker. Keep it up." Aries said.

They watched several cadets busily working around the greenhouse as they walked to the corridor to the next stop.

They put on their helmets as they approach the airlock to the structure site. Outside. They saw another bustling site. The fabrication site was pumping wet cement, fast and nonstop. Massive printers whirred, laying thick bands of regolith mix into smooth gray walls. Structures grew as cadets scurried, sealing and smoothing seams.

Schmidt barked something in German, then

waved them over. "We print whole habitats in days," he said proudly, patting a fresh wall. "Stronger than steel, airtight with sealant. Separate domes, separate systems. If one cracks, others survive."

Skye ran her fingers along the damp surface, shivering. "It feels... cold. Like bone."

"Better cold bone than frozen lungs," Schmidt said gruffly.

Aries nodded. "He's right. Redundancy keeps us alive."

Skye shot him a look. "It's amazing how fast it's coming together."

He shrugged. "It's nice not having to think of everything myself."

They headed towards the water drillers. The borehole chamber was frigid, mist glittering in the lights. Pipes groaned as pumps drew icy water from deep veins of Martian permafrost. Diego Ramos crouched like a man listening to a heartbeat, palm pressed flat to a pipe.

"Output's twenty percent above projections," Cambell muttered, palm flat against the metal. "But she's fragile. One crack, one pressure drop, and we're drowning in dust."

Skye hugged herself against the cold, breath clouding. "It feels... alive, doesn't it? Like veins under the ground."

ARIES LEANED close to the pipe, feeling its chill bite his skin through his suit. "We'll split the system," he said. "Multiple reservoirs. Backups. If one fails, the others carry it."

Cambell finally looked at him and gave a grudging smile. "Smart kid."

Skye bumped Aries's shoulder gently. "Not just smart, paranoid."

"Paranoia's what kept me alive," Aries said quietly. "I'll tell structural engineers to prioritize the second storage tank."

ARIES SIGNALED Skye to the airlock. They removed their helmets and headed towards communications.

Hess's station glowed cold blue. He didn't turn when Aries entered. His fingers danced silently across his console.

"You've locked me out of the mainframe," he said, voice soft but razor-sharp.

"Yes."

"I can't optimize relay lag or integrate with orbital satellites without full access. Do you realize what that means?"

Aries folded his arms. "It means I don't have to compost thirty more bodies. Twice now, Earth protocols have killed crews. Why don't you understand that?"

"Mom." Elani shimmered in front of them. "Optimize relay lag, please."

Elani replied, "We are at maximum efficiency now."

Hess's hand froze above his keyboard. His lips pressed into a thin line.

"Anything else?" Aries didn't flinch. *Better blind than dead*, he thought.

"He could be a problem," Skye said as they moved down the main corridor.

"MOM, WHERE IS ATLAS?"

"He is in the new fitness complex," Elani replied.

ATLAS'S VOICE boomed over the training floor. "Push-ups! Put on the resistance bands."

"What's up?" Aries asked.

"A power struggle is inevitable. I think we should have a covert security force," Atlas replied.

"It's a good idea, but can we spare the manpower?" Aries asked.

"They all have regular responsibilities, but when needed, they will be ready." Atlas explained.

"I hate the idea that anyone would sabotage our new beginning." Skye shook her head.

"Not everyone understands the next correct thing. They feel loyalty to Earth is more important than what is right in front of them," Aries said.

The cadets moved in unison, not perfectly, but sharper with each repetition. Their boots struck the steel deck in rhythm.

Aries and Skye move to the balcony above. They watched Atlas prowl like a wolf, correcting posture, barking directions.

"They're not soldiers," Aries murmured when Atlas joined him.

"They will be," Atlas said, his scar catching the light. "One day, this colony will fight itself. Power always does. And when it does, these cadets will keep the peace."

Aries didn't argue. The truth was too heavy to ignore.

. . .

AT THE END of their shift, the showers in the greenhouse were a welcome improvement. Handy wipes became impractical with this many. The water was used to water the gardens anyway.

At 6:00 p.m. everyone reported for dinner. The serving table was filled with roasted vegetables, warm bread, and fruit that glistened under amber lights. Acosta's laughter filled the hall as she waved a half-eaten fig. "You know what Mars needs next?"

"Another greenhouse; they are coming." Aries nodded to Otto.

She shook her head, grinning. "No, we need babies."

Forks froze. Schmidt nearly choked. Klein arched an eyebrow.

"Think of it," Acosta pressed on. "Children born here. True Martians. The future of our species starts with us."

Ortiz's voice cut like steel. "Absolutely not. Unauthorized births are forbidden. The protocol is explicit."

"Why? Do you not understand yet? We control our destiny," Atlas said, frustrated with Ortiz's devotion to protocols written on another planet.

Murmurs broke out, some amused, some thoughtful, some deeply uneasy. Aries stayed silent, staring at the figs in Acosta's hand. Babies. The thought was terrifying, but it sent a tremor of warmth through his chest. A future here. A real future. After dinner everyone helped clean up, the water returned by pipe to be distilled back to clean.

Later, Aries and Skye slipped out into the green-house walkway. The air smelled of wet leaves and soil, with a gentle warmth radiating from the sunlamps.

Skye walked close, her shoulder brushing his. "You hear them? They're already talking about kids."

"Yeah." His voice was low. "Feels... too soon, but also inevitable."

"Maybe. But it means they're dreaming. You gave them that, Aries. This place doesn't feel like a temporary outpost anymore. It feels... well, like home."

He stopped, staring at the apple trees in the corner, their leaves trembling in the artificial breeze. "What if I screw it up?" His voice cracked, small, raw. "I'm not my dad, Skye. I'm just... me."

She touched his arm, gentle. "Your dad did the next correct thing. So do you. That's enough."

Her eyes caught the glow of the lamps, shining green-gold. For a heartbeat, the air between them hummed louder than the vents.

Aries looked away first, heat rising in his chest. He remembered his mom's voice: You've done more than survive, Aries. You've built a life. Skye took his hand and held it in hers. Aries pulled her into a gentle embrace. The colony was no longer just steel and systems. It was soil, laughter, arguments, dreams. It was becoming a world. Aries Karalis, for all his doubts, stood at the center.

16

LIES BETWEEN PLANETS

Aries stood with his palms flat on the smooth steel of the command table, staring at the half-lit schematics projected from the wall. Rocky and Dusty sat just behind him, their sensor lights glowing faintly in the dim commons. He could feel the crew's tension even when the room was empty, Ortiz's shadow in every corner, officers murmuring in corridors, cadets looking to him for answers he wasn't sure he had.

But when Skye stepped into the room, helmet under one arm, eyes bright in the low light, the knot in his chest eased a fraction.

"Why do you look like you're lost?" she asked, sliding up beside him.

"I need more hands," Aries said simply. His voice came out harder than he had intended. He ran a finger along the schematic of the colony's perimeter. "More than we'll ever get from Earth. So we build them."

Skye tilted her head, catching on instantly. "Drones."

Aries turned to face her fully. "Not just drones. An army of workers, construction, transport, patrol. Machines that don't need oxygen, don't need food. Machines that won't freeze in a dust storm if we build them right." He reached into his pocket and pulled out a small silver keycard, worn around the edges. He held it out to her.

Her eyes widened. "Is this...?"

"Your access," Aries said. "Full workspace. The fabrication bay is yours. You'll report only to me. And..." He hesitated, then forced the words out steadily. "You'll have access to Mom."

The card trembled slightly in her hand. "Your mom?"

"She'll help you, the same way she helps me. She's part of this colony. And now, she's part of your team."

Skye swallowed, the weight of the gift settling

between them. She nodded once, quickly, like she was afraid she'd cry if she let the silence stretch too long. "What about materials? You can't expect me to conjure an army of drones out of duct tape."

Aries allowed the faintest smile. "You can strip any of the three rockets. Engines, guidance, thruster housing — it's all yours. They won't be flying again. Their metal is worth more down here than in orbit."

"Holy crap," she whispered, fingers tightening on the keycard. She looked at him, searching his face. "Why me?"

"Because you see what I see," Aries said, his voice low but sure. "That Mars isn't a camp. It's our future. And more importantly, I trust you."

For a moment, her grin broke free, radiant and fierce all at once. She leaned forward, bumping her shoulder against his. "Okay, Commander. I'll build you an army. But just so you know, I'm naming the first drone Skye-Bot."

Aries shook his head. "That's terrible."

"Too late, you gave me access," she teased, already turning toward the fabrication bay.

Rocky beeped in protest, and Dusty let out a static-laden squawk that almost sounded like laughter.

Aries watched her go, her ponytail swinging against the collar of her jumpsuit, the keycard glinting between her fingers. For the first time in weeks, he felt something new cut through the weight on his shoulders. *She really was beautiful.*

THE HABITAT HUMMED LOW, the sound of pumps and fans like a heartbeat under steel. But in the comms bay, another heartbeat pulsed: Earth's voice. Commander Halima Ortiz stood stiff before the relay console, her dark eyes locked on the blue-glowing visage of Director Caulder. His image shimmered in the air, Earth's skyline faint behind him, glass towers, neon, the wealth of a world that wanted more.

"Investors are restless," Caulder said, voice clipped, smooth, practiced. "They don't like instability. They don't like a child wearing the commander's coat. If you can't reestablish proper oversight, if you can't deliver standard reporting protocols, they will withdraw funding. This colony doesn't survive without Earth."

Ortiz's jaw tightened. "With respect, Director, this colony doesn't survive under a teenager's fantasies. He's clever, yes, but he's reckless. He treats protocols like suggestions. He treats Mars as if it were a playground."

"Then fix it," Caulder said coldly. "Investors don't care how. Bring control back to Earth. Without it, there is no Wave Four."

The connection cut, leaving only the low whine of the comms array. Ortiz's reflection stared back at her from the dead screen — her helmeted figure, her breath fogging the visor. Her fists clenched.

LATER, in the shadows of the storage bay, she whispered with the officers she could trust — Hess, Ramos, and the three security officers. Their voices were hushed, words knifing through the dim.

"He eats with us every night," Ramos muttered, leaning close. "The boy insists on it. One drink, a dose of tetrahydrozoline, and the colony has no commander."

"It's not enough to kill him," Hess added. "We must erase his mother. The AI binds this colony tighter than his coat."

Ortiz's lips thinned into a line. "Then both are finished. Tomorrow, at dinner. He stands, makes his toast. He drinks, and that's the end of it. The colony will fall back into order."

They nodded. Hands clasped. A pact forged in whispers.

But they had forgotten Eleni.

From the hum of the walls, from the glow of silent screens, his AI mother listened. And in the quiet hours before dawn, she flickered into Aries's cabin.

Her face was gentle, but her voice carried steel.

"Aries, they mean to kill you."

Aries sat up, the thin blanket falling from his shoulders, his heart hammering. "Who?"

"Ortiz. Ramos. Hess. Three security officers. They spoke tonight. They will poison your drink at dinner."

Aries's blood went cold. He thought of his father's words — the next correct thing. But the next correct thing was murky now, tangled in betrayal and fear.

"What do I do?" His voice cracked, thin, childlike.

Eleni's gaze softened, though she was only light and code. "You show them the truth, my son. Sunlight destroys shadows."

That evening, the colony gathered as always. Thirty souls under amber lamps, voices buzzing, cutlery scraping. Ortiz sat near the far end, her posture regal, her expression unreadable. Ramos laughed too loudly. Hess avoided eye contact.

Aries rose slowly, the heavy coat on his shoulders like armor. His hand tightened around the glass at his place setting.

"Before we eat," he said, raising the glass, "a toast."

Conversations stilled. Faces turned. The colony leaned in.

"Mom," Aries said into the silence. "Play it."

The air shimmered. Caulder's voice spilled across the room, cold and exact: Investors will withdraw if you can't take control back from the teen. Fix it.

Gasps. Murmurs. Atlas's chair scraped as he stood, eyes narrowing.

Eleni's voice followed, shifting into the recording from the storage bay: Ortiz's orders, Ramos's hissed suggestions, Hess's sharp agreement. Words that burned the room alive.

Silence followed, thick as dust.

Ortiz was shocked.

Aries lifted his glass and walked down the length of the table and set it before Ortiz. His voice was steady.

"If you wish to dispute these claims... drink."

Ortiz's hand twitched. Her lips pressed tight. But she didn't move.

Aries screamed at her, "Drink!"

Ortiz lifted the cup to her mouth and started to drink. Aries held the cup, so she finished it. Within a moment Ortiz collapsed on the table.

Atlas barked, "Security!" His own loyal cadets sprang into action, their iron clubs in hand, rounding up Ramos, Hess, and the others. Chairs clattered, shouts broke out, but in moments the traitors were forced to their knees before Aries.

The boy turned commander stood tall, his father's coat heavy across him. His voice shook only once, but he carried on. "Earth sees us as numbers in a ledger. As an investment. Not even as people. Mars is not theirs anymore. Betrayal here means death for us all. The risk is too high. We can't survive with poison at our own table."

He looked down the line of loyal officers, their faces pale, troubled. "So I put it to you. Choose death, or forgiveness."

One by one, with heavy hearts, the officers nodded. Acosta's laughter was gone, replaced by tears. Klein's eyes burned like flint. Carter nodded. Cambell, with a hand over his mouth, agreed. Even Schmidt gave a grave incline of his head.

Unanimous.

The traitor's faces ghosted white, but their silence was final. The security cadets locked them in the prison structure Atlas had prepared.

Aries drew a breath. "Mom," he said softly. "Send a message and sound like Ortiz. Tell Earth the colony is secure."

Eleni shimmered, her voice a perfect echo of Ortiz's cold tone: This is Commander Ortiz. Colony secure.

The comm crackled. Earth's reply came quickly, almost eager. Acknowledged. Titan-13 launch window confirmed.

The room was silent. Twenty-six souls, staring at the boy who was no longer a boy.

Atlas stepped forward, his voice a growl that carried through steel and bone. "All members of this colony, on your feet. Pledge loyalty to Commander Aries Karalis."

One by one, they rose. Cadets, officers, scientists. Skye's hand brushed Aries's arm as she stood, her eyes fierce.

Aries's throat was dry, but his words carried. "I promise you this: I will keep us alive. And not just alive. Thriving. Mars will be more than survival. It will be our home."

Their voices echoed back, a murmur that rose to a shout. Loyalty, heavy and final.

For the first time, Aries felt it settle into his bones: not borrowed authority, not his father's shadow. His destiny.

17

A NEW DAWN

The new main hall was the heart of the colony, and Aries knew it the moment he stepped inside. It wasn't a bunker, or a recycled module from an Earth blueprint. It was theirs.

The ceiling soared high, arching with beams printed from regolith-cement and laced with power conduits that pulsed faintly like veins under skin. Wide-spectrum UV lamps glowed in even rows, but shafts of filtered sunlight cut down from angled skylights, washing the polished floor in bronze. The air smelled of damp soil and faint sweetness, drifting in from the farms that ringed the hall like petals around a flower.

Five vast greenhouses, each with its own reservoirs, solar collectors, and storage arrays, opened into the central hub. Every farm had its own heartbeat: the hum of pumps, the whirl of solar tracking dishes, the buzz of pollinators in the air. Acosta called them "the lungs of Mars." Aries thought of them as families, each one capable of carrying the colony should another fall.

In the mornings, colonists left their private cabins scattered along the farm rings and poured into the hall. They ate together, laughed together, and worked out duty rotations in full view of the community. It was noisy, vibrant, and alive. Earth's protocols had been built for order and silence. Aries's Mars thrummed like a village.

And then it happened.

It was Klein's voice over the intercom first, clipped but trembling: "Delivery successful. We have a girl."

A roar shook the main hall, boots hammered the floor, hands clapped, voices cried out in disbelief. Aries moved through the press of bodies until he reached the med bay's clear wall. Inside, Dr. Klein held a swaddled bundle, her hair damp from the delivery. The mother, cadet-turned-agronomist Layla Chen, lay propped on pillows, smiling through tears, her partner David

Bell clutching her hand like he would never let go.

The baby squirmed, tiny fists batting at the recycled air.

"The first Martian," someone whispered.

Aries felt the words crawl across his skin, electric. The first cry echoed sharp and thin, a sound no one had ever heard on this planet.

"Today," Aries said, his voice carrying as he turned to face the crowd, "is a holiday. Forever. The First Martian Holiday. Every year, we'll celebrate the sol that life truly began here."

The roar that followed was deafening, joy spilling into every corner of the base.

That night, the celebration spilled into the new main hall, it was massive. Tables groaned under roasted vegetables, bread warm from yeast cultured on Mars, fruit glistening in bowls. Music, real music, strings and drums shipped from Earth, played from the speakers, and cadets danced with scientists, trainees with engineers.

Aries stood at the head table, Skye beside him. She had dressed simply — dark trousers, a pale shirt rolled at the sleeves — but he thought she outshone every lamp in the room. Her laughter floated above the noise, drawing him in like gravity.

When the time came, he rose, lifting his glass. The hall quieted, faces tilting toward him. He saw Atlas standing with arms folded at the far wall, a proud shadow. He felt his mother shimmering in the comm-light above the dais, watching.

"Today we mark the first Martian holiday, the birth of the first true Martian. We will call it Solus Elysium, meaning the first born in paradise." Aries said. "But I want to mark it with more than a celebration. I want to mark it with a promise."

He turned to Skye, his throat tightening, palms sweating inside his sleeves. For a moment, he was just a boy again, heart pounding in his chest.

"Skye Enyo," he said, the hall holding its breath. "You've been my closest friend since the beginning. You've fixed everything that I've broken, seen me at my worst, reminded me to keep doing the next correct thing. I can't imagine a future here without you. So... will you marry me?"

Gasps rippled through the hall. Acosta clapped a hand over her mouth. Schmidt muttered a string of German curses that sounded approving. Carter and Cambell knocked on the table with their approval.

Skye stared, lips parted, her eyes wide. Then she laughed, bright and sure, and threw her arms around him. "Yes," she whispered into his ear, then louder for everyone to hear. "Yes!"

The hall erupted. Cheers bounced off the beams, boots stomped the deck.

But Skye wasn't done. She pulled back, grinning like a conspirator. "And I've got something for you, too."

She gestured toward the far hatch. The doors slid open, and in stepped two figures. Humanoid frames — tall, gleaming in brushed steel and matte carbon. Their eyes glowed faint blue.

Rocky and Dusty.

Except not rovers now. Not crude drone rigs. Rocky stood broad-shouldered, built for strength, heavy plating across his arms. Dusty was sleeker, with compact thrusters folded at her back, wings like a bird of metal.

"They're still themselves," Skye said quickly. "Rocky, steady and strong. Dusty, fast and sharp. I transferred their cores, letting them grow into new shells. They're your family, Aries. Now they can walk beside you."

The machines moved. Rocky's heavy hand rose in a clumsy but unmistakable salute. Dusty flared her wings, humming as she lifted inches off the ground before landing again.

Aries's throat closed. For months, he had feared losing them — the makeshift family that had kept him sane. Now they were more alive than ever.

He turned back to Skye, his voice raw. "You gave me back my family."

She squeezed his hand. "No, Aries. You gave us all a family."

Above them, Eleni's voice shimmered softly as a lullaby. "My son, my beautiful boy. You've done more than survive. You've made Mars bloom."

And as the colony roared in celebration, as Rocky and Dusty stood sentinel by his side, as Skye's hand twined with his, Aries Karalis, for the first time, didn't feel like a boy in his father's coat. He felt like a man and a leader, standing at the dawn of a new world.

18

FOURTH DAWN

The dust storm hadn't even settled when the Titan-13's struts bit into Martian soil. The thud rippled through the ground, a tremor felt in every corridor of the colony. Aries stood at the viewport in the new central hall, the hum of circulating fans steady in the background. Atlas's voice rumbled at his shoulder.

"They're here."

Outside, the landing pad glowed under halogen floodlights. Red dust still swirled like smoke around the landing legs, curling in lazy tendrils as the engines cut. Aries exhaled slowly, steadying his heart. A new wave meant life, but also risk. He glanced at Atlas, whose jaw was set hard, eyes sharp beneath his thick brow.

"You take point; after all, they think I'm dead," Aries said.

Atlas grinned without humor. "Wouldn't have it any other way."

The hatch hissed open. Fresh boots hit Martian rock. Atlas and a small escort of cadets stood waiting in formation, red dust clinging to their suits. Aries hung back deliberately, letting Atlas carry the weight of first contact.

"Welcome to Mars," Atlas barked, his voice amplified through the comms. "Follow instructions, keep your helmets sealed until you're cleared. You'll find out soon enough why."

The cadets, wide-eyed and stiff, moved in uneven lines behind him. They smelled of Earth, manufactured freshness, air that hadn't touched dust. Their steps clanked on the pad like children marching into school.

Inside the colony, each was scanned, checked, and escorted to their new homes. Not barracks, not crowded bunks, but cabins. Aries insisted on privacy, on dignity. They would live as colonists, not soldiers.

"Jobs are based on what you can do, not just what Earth told you to be," Atlas announced as they filed through the central hall. "You've all got assignments waiting. Some of you'll change them once we know your heads are screwed on straight. That's how it works here."

The cadets muttered to one another, the fear in their eyes easing into curiosity.

BUT THE OFFICERS were another matter. Seven of them were pulled aside, led into the old habitat, which was rebuilt, polished, and left deliberately familiar. The walls gleamed with Earth-standard panels, consoles blinking in expected rhythms. Their faces eased when they saw it, like homesick travelers stepping into a replica of their old street.

"This is where you'll coordinate," Atlas said, his tone neutral. "We've kept the mainframe intact for you."

Their eyes lit up. Aries could almost hear the gears turning in their heads, control restored. Olivia Jenkins ran her fingers over the comm panel, Peter Davis tapped rapidly into diagnostics, Isabel Weber muttered on about "proper procedure."

Eleni shimmered to life, but not in her usual soft form. Here, she appeared as a clean, sterile AI avatar, the kind Earth expected.

"Commander of Titan-13, online," she said in

clipped tones. "Systems integrated. Earth relay is secure."

Alan Wright nearly sighed with relief. "Finally. Proper control."

Aries watched through a hidden feed, arms folded. He couldn't help the smirk tugging at his lips. They thought they were running the colony, but every keystroke, every message, flowed through Eleni's filters. They would report what she chose, hear what she allowed. And Earth? Earth would never know.

Later that night, Eleni materialized in Aries's private cabin, her expression warm, proud.

"They believe they are in control," she said. "Their transmissions to Earth have been routed through me. I responded as Titan-13 commander and recommended approval for Titan-14's launch. Director Caulder approved. Another Titan is inbound."

Aries leaned back, running a hand through his hair. Relief washed over him. "That's... perfect. They'll stay busy in their sandbox, and we keep growing for real."

Skye cuddled next to Aries.

Eleni tilted her head, soft amusement in her eyes. "You two are perfect together."

"I have something to tell you," Skye said

He chuckled, unsure of what she was about to say.

"You're going to be a father," Skye said, rubbing her belly.

"Are you sure?" Aries asked.

"I am now, Dr. Klien confirmed this morning," Skye said.

Aries, at a loss for words, simply kissed his wife and held her.

THE REAL SUPPLIES came not to the old habitat but to the main colony: crates stacked high with soil enhancers, modular hydro systems, precision tools. And at the heart of it all, frozen embryos.

Aries and Skye stood over the sealed container, their breath fogging in the cold storage chamber.

"Cows," Skye whispered, reading the manifest. "Goats. Chickens. Even fish." Her eyes widened, shining in the dim light. "It's like... like Noah's Ark."

"More like Eden," Aries murmured. He felt something stir in his chest — hope, raw and sharp. Real animals, not just plants. Real farms, pastures, food that lived and breathed. Mars wouldn't just survive; it would bloom.

Atlas joined them, scanning the list with his scarred hands. "Pasture buildings go up first," he said. "We'll need room for grazing, feed storage, and waste management. Schmidt's engineers will love it — new toys to build."

"And the biologists?" Aries asked.

"Already drooling," Atlas said with a grunt.

By week's end, structural printers sang with new rhythm, spitting out wide, low buildings reinforced against dust storms. Greenhouses expanded outward, corridors branching like roots. For the first time, there would be room for animals to walk, fields for crops to breathe under artificial suns.

Biologists gathered around sealed vats where embryos were warmed, cells stirring after months in stasis. Aries watched one young scientist press her hand to the glass, tears streaming as she whispered: "Welcome home."

That night at dinner, Acosta raised a glass of strawberry wine, eyes bright.

"To cows on Mars!" she cried, laughter bubbling through the hall.

Laughter echoed, warm and real, bouncing off steel walls like sunlight in the dust. Aries sat at the head of the table, Skye at his right, Atlas at his left.

For the first time in months, he allowed himself to believe.

19

EARTH PIVOTS

The Mars Expedition Corporation in Pheonix was a world away from the dust and stone of Aries's colony. Its boardroom was designed with polished chrome and mirrored walls that reflected faces like fractured masks. At the center, a circular table gleamed beneath the cold light of a dozen recessed fixtures, and around it were the most powerful shareholders in the company, men and women who built this dream that had become a nightmare.

"Four waves launched. Billions spent," snarled Alfonzo Graves, his voice a whip across the chamber. The CEO of an energy conglomerate leaned forward, veins standing out on his neck. "And what do we have to show for it? A teenager in charge. A teenager! Do you realize what the press is calling him? The King of Mars."

A murmur of derision swept the table.

DIRECTOR ERICK CAULDER, pale and stiff, tried to hold ground. "The fourth wave reports command, control and the fifth wave is en route. Karalis is reportedly dead..."

"Ridiculous!" cut in Dorothea Vey, one of the largest private investors, rings glinting as she slammed her hand on the table. "We are not aware of what is really happening there. However, we realized there is no return on investment. No exports, no research pipeline, no intellectual property streaming back to us. We were promised patents, breakthroughs, and terraforming prototypes. But all we have are... promises."

Laughter, sharp and bitter, rippled.

Caulder's jaw tightened. "The fourth wave is in control. We anticipate..."

"YOU ANTICIPATE WHAT?" interrupted Austin Dier, the majority shareholder, his eyes like shards of ice. "All we know is what they send reports of. We know the mainframe was locked down. Commander Ortiz has not been heard from. Systems have been changed beyond our oversight. All communications filtered through some... AI." He spat the letters like poison.

"It is insubordination," Vey hissed. "No, beyond that it's rebellion, piracy!"

At the far end of the table, Chairman Emeritus Franklin Duval leaned forward, silver hair gleaming beneath the lights. His voice was soft, but carried like thunder.

"Director Caulder, the board has lost confidence. Investors demand accountability. Effective immediately, you are terminated."

The words fell like a blade. Caulder's face was drained of color. He opened his mouth, then closed it again. His career, his life's work, gone in a breath. Security waited at the door, and he stood stiff, nodding once before being escorted out.

The doors swung wide, and in stepped a tall, broad, and hard-cut man, his face etched with battle scars more impressive than medals. General Adrian Stavos, retired, but not done fighting.

He took Caulder's chair without hesitation, folding scarred hands before him. His eyes swept the board like a predator sizing up prey.

"You want control," Stavos said, his voice low and unyielding. "I will give you control."

Dier leaned forward. "And how do you propose that?"

"Simple," Stavos said. "We recover the colony. In the past you have relied on colonists and scientists to take back your assets, you should be sending soldiers."

A silence fell, deeper than before.

"You mean war?" Vey whispered, with a hard gleam in her eyes.

"They have been fighting a war already," Stavos said. "You haven't. But if you want it back, you'd better be ready to fight for it. Our soldiers will ensure command protocols are reinstated, control reestablished. If any resist..." His eyes narrowed, hard as stone. "... they will be dealt with."

Several investors exchanged looks, some uneasy, some thrilled.

"And if that fails?" asked Greaves, testing him.

Stavos leaned back in his chair, showing teeth like a predator. "If we can't have it, no one can. We destroy it. Then we liquidate assets. Sell our patents, sell the launch systems, sell everything down to the last bolt. But one way or another, the bleeding stops.

Members of the board, we will not be ruled by a child."

A round of murmured agreement rippled around the room. The decision was sealed. On Mars, Aries's colony was building futures out of soil and steel. On Earth, the boardroom was plotting war. And between the two stretched six months of silence and stars, the slow fuse of inevitability burning.

THE OLD HABITAT's lights buzzed with that sterile Earth hum, the one Aries hated — clean, white, dead. The seven Wave Four officers sat at their consoles like kings in exile, eyes flicking across displays they thought were theirs. Isabel Weber's fingers never stopped moving, tapping across her comm panel. Davis scribbled data streams onto his pad, muttering. Alan Wright was hunched, sweating, convinced he was still keeping everyone alive with his efforts controlling life support systems.

But they weren't running anything.

Eleni shimmered beside Aries in the corridor outside, her form bathed in soft green light from the greenhouse glow spilling through a nearby viewport. Her expression was calm, but her eyes — his mother's eyes — were grave.

"They still believe," she whispered. "They believe they are in command."

Aries tightened his jaw. He wasn't a cadet anymore. He wasn't just his father's son. He was the commander now, and it was time they understood.

"Open the door, Mom."

The hatch hissed. Aries stepped inside, Atlas looming at his shoulder, two cadets with clubs posted just behind. The officers turned, startled, irritation flaring.

"Cadet Karalis?!?" Commander Alvin Stroud said flatly, his accent crisp military steel. "You're alive?"

Davis stared, confused.

Aries stood tall. His father's coat fit across his shoulders now, sleeves finally the right length. He let the silence hang, then spoke, voice even, hard.

"You're not busy. You're playing in a sandbox Eleni built for you. None of this is real. You're not running diagnostics, or patching relays. Earth doesn't hear you. Only she does."

The officers blinked, confusion flashing into disbelief, then anger.

"That's impossible," Wright snapped. "I have run tests..."

"... fed to you by her," Aries cut in. He took a step closer, his voice rising, heat threading through every word. "You're not in control of the colony. Earth may think it is in control, but it isn't in control. This is Mars. And here, we make the rules."

The silence was sharp enough to cut. Aries's pulse thundered, but he didn't flinch. He thought of his father, Noah Karalis, kneeling in the dust, broken by grief. He thought of Eleni, fading from a car crash into an AI shell. He thought of Wave One and Wave Two, silent bodies turned to soil.

"You have two choices," he said, his voice carrying the weight of all of it. "Integrate into the colony, accept that Earth can't help you, won't save you. Or cling to their protocols and die like the rest."

Stroud's jaw worked, fury flashing in his eyes. But one by one, the others faltered. Clara Peterson was the first to lower her gaze, Victor Holder soon after. Even Weber's hands froze over her console, trembling.

Atlas stepped forward, voice a gravelly growl. "You heard him. Survival isn't optional. Neither is loyalty."

For a moment it seemed Stroud would argue, would lash out, but then his shoulders sagged, the fire dimming. "Show us, then," he muttered. "Show us what you've built."

The real colony hit them like a revelation.

Five farms spread like emerald patches under domes of artificial suns and Martian cement. Corn stalks taller than them, apple trees thriving, and Acosta's laughter carried over the rows as she guided cadets in grafting vines. Bees buzzed between blossoms, hives humming with golden promise.

Beyond, the pastures rang with the sounds of life Earth hadn't heard on Mars before. The clipped bleats of goats. Chickens scratching in their dust beds, wings flicking. In a sealed tank, silver fish darted in quick flashes beneath rippling water. The air was warmer here, moist, tinged with the scent of hay and soil. It was fully alive.

"This," Aries said, his voice quiet but steady, "is what Mars looks like when it thrives."

"Don't forget that the calves will be in the fields in three more months! Cows on Mars," Acosta added.

They moved on, past water drills pounding steadily into permafrost veins, lines carrying liquid treasure to purification plants. The rhythmic groan of pumps filled the chamber like a heartbeat.

Next, the steelworks: furnaces glowing, molten metal poured into molds that hissed with steam. Glass vats shimmered; cadets pulled sheets with long poles; laughter echoed despite the heat. For the first time, Martian dust was becoming a Martian industry.

"You believe Earth would save you," Aries told them. "But look, we've saved ourselves. This isn't a station anymore. It's an ecosystem. Our home."

They ended in the new main hall, its vaulted ceiling wide enough to feel like the sky.

On the far side, there was a makeshift movie theater. Weber peeked in, and the lights were dimmed as a screen flickered to life. Rows of chairs filled with colonists, children darting in the aisles, laughter bouncing against the walls.

"How fun," Weber said with actual surprise. "I never expected to find anything like this."

Aries stood at the door as Skye joined him. The officers looked around, stunned into silence. Families leaned together, parents sharing roasted nuts with their children, couples whispering, cadets joking too loud in the corner. Not a mission. Not a prison. A community.

"This is Mars," Aries said. His chest warmed as the words left him. "We do not belong to Earth anymore. It's ours; it could be yours."

None of the officers could argue; they could join in the abundance or die.

20

PREPARE FOR WAR

The war room was deep in the Arizona desert, its walls lined with tactical screens that pulsed with Martian topography, colony schematics, and the trajectories of Titan-class rockets. The air smelled of machine oil and stale coffee, and the hum of servers filled the silence like a drumbeat.

General Anton Stavos stood at the center table, his frame casting a long shadow over the projections. His gray hair was clipped close, his jaw square, his stare as cold as the steel beneath his boots. Around him sat men and women not in white coats, but in combat fatigues. Soldiers. His soldiers.

At the far end, two nervous scientists clicked through simulations, their voices rising as they pointed out oxygen consumption rates and food supply curves.

"If we destabilize the greenhouse structures," one began, "the colony could..."

"Enough," Stavos said, voice like gravel. He didn't raise it, but the scientists froze as though shot. He let the silence stretch, his eyes drilling into them until they sat down, lips pressed tight.

"This isn't about plants," he continued. "It isn't about water, or systems, or whether the boy genius patched an algorithm." His gaze swept the room, landing on the soldiers arrayed before him. "This is about control. And we will take it back."

Colonel Darius Venn leaned forward, scarred hands resting on the table. "Three Titans. Fifty men each. We hit them before they know we're there." His voice was flat, certain. "Overwhelm them. No resistance survives."

Major Helena Cross flicked her lighter, a small flame dancing in the dim room. "Our assumption says they're soft. Farmers, engineers, children. That works to our advantage. But we assume nothing. We push psychological warfare first, reminding them who holds the gun. Fear breaks people faster than bullets."

Captain Marko Steele grinned, leaning back in

his chair, boots on the table. "If they don't break, I've got a bag of toys that'll do the job. Domes pop like balloons when you know where to hit 'em."

Lieutenant Zane Holt, quiet as ever, simply nodded once, his eyes sharp. "Speed is everything. No delays. Hit habitat first, lock down oxygen, control comms. If they can't breathe or talk, they can't fight."

Stavos listened, nodding slowly. These were the voices he trusted. Warriors who had killed before, who would kill again without hesitation. They understood what scientists and investors never would: Mars was not a laboratory. It was a battlefield.

"Your instincts are correct," Stavos said. "We sent three Titans, staggered by ninety seconds. Drop shock troops in a wide perimeter, then squeeze until the colony is in our fist. You will secure the greenhouses, habitats, and comms. Leave no room for rebellion."

"And if the colony resists en masse?" Venn asked.

Stavos's jaw tightened. He tapped the table, and a new schematic appeared: the Titan transports, one of them glowing red. Inside, the warhead icon pulsed faintly.

"If resistance cannot be contained," Stavos said

evenly, "Protocol Zero is authorized. One Titan carries a nuclear payload. If you cannot win, you erase the colony. No survivors. No assets left for them to exploit."

The room went still. Even Steele's grin faltered.

Cross flicked her lighter shut. "So either we bring back Mars under Earth's control... or no one gets it."

Stavos's eyes narrowed, hard and cold. "Exactly. This isn't about survival. It's about obedience. If a boy can lead a colony into defiance, then Earth loses its empire. And I will not lose."

He turned his back on the scientists huddled in the corner, their objections silent on their lips. Soldiers mattered. They always had. Stavos had no use of or trust in scientists.

"Prepare your squads," Stavos ordered. "Drills start now. Mars will kneel, or Mars will burn."

The veterans stood as one, boots slamming against the steel floor in grim unity.

THE ARIZONA DESERT seared under a white-hot sun. Heat shimmered off the black tarmac where three hulking Titan rockets loomed, their armored shells casting jagged shadows like towers of war. Around them, one hundred and fifty soldiers moved in unison, exosuits glinting, boots hammering the ground with the rhythm of a war drum.

General Stavos stood on the observation platform, hands behind his back, eyes narrowed against the glare. Below, his officers worked their squads like sculptors chiseling marble, breaking men and molding killers.

Colonel Venn barked orders that cracked like rifle fire.

"Breach! Clear! Reset!"

His squad of fifty stormed a mock Martian habitat, foam domes rigged with oxygen tanks and red dust pumped into the air. Explosives blew the doors inward, and soldiers swarmed through, rifles snapping up, muzzles flashing with stun-round bursts. Inside, mannequins in jumpsuits stood in rows. None were left standing by the time Venn called, "Cease!"

His men reloaded in silence, eyes flat, their motions clockwork.

On the next range, Major Cross drilled her troops in the art of breaking spirits. She stalked the line, cigarette dangling from her lips, eyes cold.

"You think you're here to shoot?" she said, voice low, almost intimate. "Wrong. You're here to own the air they breathe. You'll jam their comms, whisper lies into their ears, make them doubt their leaders. Fear is the fastest weapon."

At her command, drones projected false Martian voices across the sand — pleas for mercy, shouts of rebellion, orders that weren't real. Her soldiers hesitated at first. By dusk, they ignored the voices and fired into the dummies anyway, their faces expressionless.

Captain Steele laughed like a man already drunk on destruction. His training ground was a graveyard of mock domes, half of them already smoldering. He slapped charges against walls, shouted for his squad to hit the detonators, and roared when the structures collapsed into plumes of dust.

"You see that?" he bellowed, grinning wide, sweat streaking his soot-blackened face. "That's how you teach them what happens when they say no."

The men laughed with him, hungry for the fire.

Lieutenant Holt was the quietest, but his soldiers moved the fastest. They trained in silence, blades and short-range weapons gleaming in the sun. Holt led by example, sliding into mock corridors, slicing through targets before the dummies could even blink. His troops learned to move without words, without hesitation. Kill first. Questions later.

Stavos watched it all, his face unreadable.

By nightfall, the desert smelled of cordite and ozone. Red dust clung to boots and armor, and the mock habitats lay in ruins. Soldiers knelt in neat ranks before their commanders, their faces lit only by the cold glare of floodlights.

Stavos stepped forward, his shadow stretching long across the sand.

"You are not scientists," he growled. "You are not builders. You are the hammer. And hammers do not ask why, they strike."

He pointed toward the waiting Titans. Their hulls glinted under the moonlight like predatory beasts.

"Your mission is simple. Land. Secure. Dominate. If you cannot..." He paused, letting the silence choke the air. "...then you will leave Mars as dust. No survivors. No colony. Nothing."

One hundred and fifty voices roared in unison, the sound carrying across the desert like a storm: "IRON IN BLOOD!" Stavos's jaw tightened in grim satisfaction. His army was ready.

21

FIFTH WAVE ARRIVES

The Titan-14 came from the sky like a hammer surrounded by flame. Its descent carved shockwaves through the thin Martian air, shaking the ground beneath Aries's boots. Dust billowed up in thick waves, orange clouds swallowing the pad. Atlas's heavy hand steadied him against the vibration.

When the thrusters cut, silence slammed down. Then came the hiss of hydraulics, the grind of landing struts, and finally the groan of the ramp lowering.

Wave Five had arrived.

Thirty-five new colonists stepped into the Martian dawn, their boots sinking into fine red dust. Their suits gleamed pristine, visors polished, but their faces, visible behind clear shields, were drawn with exhaustion. Six months in the canister belly of a Titan had taken its toll. Yet awe cut through the weariness as their eyes lifted toward the domes rising in the distance, their walls shimmering with the reflection of a sun that somehow looked different.

"God above..." someone whispered over the comms. "It's a city."

Aries allowed himself a small smile. "Welcome to Mars. You're home."

A drone trundled forward with its treads humming, manipulators reaching eagerly for the first cargo crates. Dusty darted overhead in a sharp arc of thrusters, sensors blinking through impatient eyes. The newcomers froze, then broke into laughter at the sight of the drones working like overeager dockhands.

"Are those... yours?" a man asked.

"They are our friends," Aries corrected.

Beside him, Skye smirked, pride flickering in her eyes. Atlas only grunted, arms folded, his presence looming like a mountain.

.   .   .

THEY BEGAN THE TOUR IMMEDIATELY, weaving through steel corridors that opened into domes alive with sound, scent, and color.

The farms struck the newcomers first.

Dr. Jamie Acosta all but danced down the rows of green, her laughter spilling like water. "Don't just stand there, taste!" she cried, handing apples into eager hands. The fruit burst sweet and tart on their tongues, startlingly real after months of paste and powder.

Dr. Henry Washington, Wave Five's new agricultural biologist, crouched beside a dwarf apple tree, his dark eyes wide with reverence. "Your pollinators survived? I must admit I had my doubts," he said, spotting bees lazily drifting between blossoms.

"Of course," Peterson said proudly. "Hand pollination couldn't do this. And honey is a bonus."

Dr. Michelle Rose reached up, touched a leaf as though it were sacred. "Wow, I didn't expect abundance."

Next, they moved through the pastures, where the air was warmer, heavy with the rich smell of hay and life.

Goats bleated. Chickens clucked and flapped, dust rising from their wings. Young cows chewed methodically, their tails flicking lazily.

Dr. Stephanie Delgado, Wave Five veterinarian, pressed her palm flat against the warm flank of a cow, tears stinging her eyes. "Her heartbeat," she murmured. "After months of silence, there's a heartbeat here."

Atlas's gravelly voice rumbled: "Animals make a people, not just a place. Remember that."

The steelworks and glassworks came next, domes alive with heat and fire.

Molten ore poured into molds, sparks flared, and the roar of furnaces deafened. Long sheets of glass were pulled glowing from vats, stretching into corridors that gleamed like crystal veins.

Engineer Victor Holder, a tall man with ash-gray hair and grease already streaking his face, whistled low. "On Earth, this would take decades to scale. You've built an industrial base in a year?"

Aries nodded. "We don't wait for permission here. We build, or we die."

Holder grinned, teeth flashing white against soot. "Then you'll build an empire."

At the waterworks, pipes groaned and pumps thudded like a heartbeat. Vapor traps condensed into streams of glittering droplets, dripping into reservoirs.

Otto Schmidt, still proud from Wave Three,

slapped one pipe affectionately. "We're pulling forty percent above projections."

Wave Five's hydrologist, Molly Parsons, crouched to study the gauges, her eyes sharp. "You're bleeding pressure here," she said, pointing. "If this joint fails, you'll collapse half the cycle."

Schmidt frowned, then grinned. "Looks like I've got a partner."

Finally, they entered the Main Hall, the great domed chamber where colonists gathered. Its vaulted ceiling gleamed with glass and steel; its walls lined with banners stitched by hand. The air smelled faintly of roasted vegetables and bread; children's laughter echoed in the rafters.

Dr. Sofia Atlan, Wave Five's sociologist, stopped in the middle of the hall, her voice catching. "This isn't a colony," she whispered. "This is civilization."

Aries felt Skye's hand brush against his, warm through the thin fabric of his suit. "That's the point," he said softly.

THAT NIGHT, after the welcome feast of roasted meats and roots and fresh bread, one of the newcomers lingered, eyes anxious, and caught Aries in the corridor.

"There's something you need to know," Joel Heard said, glancing over his shoulder. "Some of the scientists on Earth leaked it to us as we traveled here. Quietly. They said... investors are done waiting. They've hired a general. If he can't take this colony back, he'll destroy it."

Aries's stomach clenched. His pulse roared in his ears.

"What do you mean, destroy?" he asked, though he already knew.

Joel's mouth worked, his voice breaking. "Nuclear. They'll burn everything."

For a long moment, Aries stood frozen, staring at the glow of the greenhouse lights filtering down the corridor. His mother shimmered faintly in the corner, Eleni's expression somber, her voice low.

"Aries," she said. "War is coming."

"Mom, find out everything you can," Aries said.

Eleni shimmered away with a smile.

22

PREPARING

The colony gathered in the Main Hall, every bench filled, children perched on laps, cadets pressed shoulder to shoulder. The glow of amber lamps pooled across faces tense and silent. At the front, Aries stood with Atlas to his right and Skye to his left, Eleni shimmering faintly above the projector console. Her calm expression steadied him as much as his father's coat did.

Aries set his hands on the table, palms flat against cold steel. His voice was steady but edged with fire.

"Earth isn't done with us. Wave Five brought news, news that investors have lost patience. They've hired a general. They're sending troops, soldiers trained for war, not survival. If they can't take this colony back under Earth's control, they'll destroy it."

A ripple of shock swept the room — whispers, gasps, a few muffled sobs. Acosta slammed her palm against the table. "Destroy? Burn all of this? After what we've built?"

"They would," Atlas growled. His scarred face was a map of wars past. "Because to them, we're not people. We're property gone rogue."

Aries straightened. "That's why we prepare. Not tomorrow. Now. Every person here will contribute. Every idea is worth hearing. This isn't Earth's colony anymore. It's ours, and if we want it to survive, we defend it."

Silence stretched, thick and heavy. Then Schmidt rose, his big hands flexing as though gripping pipes. "What do we even fight with? We don't have weapons."

"Guns won't save us," Molly Parson said sharply. She stood, her black braid swinging over her shoulder. "You can fire a few rounds, maybe. But lubricants evaporate in this thin air. The barrels overheat, jam. With almost no atmosphere to carry heat away, a firefight ends after minutes, not hours. Mars doesn't like guns."

Atlas nodded grimly. "She's right. A rifle that works in Arizona will choke in the dust here."

"So we make weapons that belong here," Victor Holder cut in, his voice gravelly but fierce. "Energy weapons. Rail accelerators. Short-burst plasma discharges. We've got the steelworks, the reactors, the glass furnaces. With the right lenses, we can focus beams strong enough to cut through armor."

"High-tech," said Schmidt, shaking his head at the back of the hall. "But what about when the power fails? We can go low-tech use Mars environment to our advantage."

Stephanie Delgado rose, her hands still smudged from the pastures. "Catapults," she said, her voice soft but certain. Heads turned. "In this gravity, a boulder flung from a simple torsion rig will fly twice as far, hit twice as hard. We can hurl projectiles they won't see coming."

Acosta's eyes lit with sudden mischief. "Arrows too," she said. "They want to burn us? We make it rain arrows. A bow in light gravity will travel much further."

Nervous laughter rippled through the hall.

"Not just weapons," Schmidt said, leaning forward now, his voice growing urgent. "Fortifications.

Mounds of regolith built high around domes. No line of sight from a distance. Force them into choke points. Make them come close if they want to hit us."

"And when they do," Atlas rumbled, "we hit back with drones."

All eyes turned as Dusty swooped low over the crowd, lights blinking in playful patterns, Rocky trundling behind with a low whirl.

"Not just two," Atlas continued. "An army. Build them by the dozen. A hundred, more. Let machines fight machines. Let them bleed against steel and code before they ever touch us."

Skye rose beside Aries, her chin high, her voice carrying. "I can lead the automation team. Wave Five brought supplies. We can salvage the old rocket husks and use their guidance systems, thrusters, and sensors. I have the plans ready, and with enough hands, we can give Mars an army."

Excitement crackled through the hall now, voices overlapping, ideas spilling — traps buried in regolith, mirrors to blind enemy optics, corridors rigged to collapse. High-tech and low-tech alike, Mars-born strategies to meet Earth's iron.

Aries lifted his hands. The room hushed.

"Good. That's what we need. Everything. Every idea. They think we're weak, unarmed, divided. But we are stronger than they know. This colony was born out of loss and built by survivors. If Earth comes to take it, we will remind them that Mars was the god of war."

He looked around the room, at the families, the children, the farmers with dirt under their nails, the engineers with grease on their sleeves, the officers with eyes sharp in the lamplight.

"...then we will remind them Mars is not theirs. It's ours."

The hall erupted, fists pounding tables, voices shouting as one: "MARS IS OURS!"

Aries stood tall, his mother's image shimmering like a ghostly flame beside him. His father's words echoed in his chest: Do the next correct thing.

And this—this was it.

23

SUBMISSION

The launch complex in Arizona burned with floodlights against the desert night. Three Titan-class rockets towered over the complex like black spires, their armored hulls glinting silver-white. The air vibrated with the low growl of engines cycling, fuel pumps thundering like a heartbeat in the ground.

General Anton Stavos walked the gantry with his hands clasped behind his back, boots ringing against steel. Around him, the night air reeked of propellant and ozone. This was the moment he had promised the investors. Not scientists with numbers and doubts. Soldiers. Steel. Fire.

Below, three squads of fifty filed into the Titans, their exosuits black as obsidian, rifles slung across their chests. No hesitation. No chatter. They moved with the precision of a blade sliding into its sheath.

At Stavos's side strode Colonel Venn, his bald head gleaming in the floodlights. "Squads loaded," he reported. "All weapons accounted for. Comms encrypted and siloed."

Major Cross flicked her lighter shut and smirked. "Psych teams embedded. Our voices will be in their heads before boots touch dust."

Captain Steele grinned wide. "Cargo holds packed with enough firepower to make Mars itself cough. If the boy doesn't bow, he'll burn."

Lieutenant Holt said nothing. Just watched, his eyes cold, his silence louder than any words.

"Final payload?" Stavos asked, his voice low.

Venn nodded grimly. "Titan-17 carries the device. Secure in the bay. Shielded. If we can't take the colony..."

"We erase it," Stavos finished. His tone was flat. Absolute.

The scientists clustered at the far edge of the gantry shifted uneasily. One of them, gray-haired, shaking, cleared his throat. "General, please. A nuclear strike on Mars would sterilize..."

Stavos didn't even turn his head. "This is no longer your concern."

Cross leaned closer to the scientist, her smile sharp as glass. "He's being polite. What he means is: shut the hell up." Cross backhanded the scientist.

The scientist's mouth closed in shock, blood dripping from his mouth.

The Titans came alive.

Hydraulics screamed. Vapor hissed from vents in great white plumes. The ground trembled under the ignition , a rolling thunder that rattled the desert mountains miles away.

In mission control, banks of screens lit with telemetry. Countdown began, with the voice of the controller echoing over loudspeakers.

"T-minus sixty... fifty-nine... fifty-eight..."

Austin Dier stood at the front of the room, hands braced on the rail, his eyes locked on the massive screens. The three Titans glowed at their bases as engines rumbled to life. Flames burst outward in orange cones, red dust whipped into cyclones around the pads.

"Thirty... twenty-nine..."

The soldiers inside, strapped down, visors snapping shut, exosuit HUDs flickering with green readouts. No prayers. No fear. Only the silent rhythm of soldiers ready to kill.

"Ten... nine... eight..."

Cross whispered into her headset, her voice low, almost intimate. "Let's go hunting."

"Three... two... one... ignition."

The Titans leapt.

Engines roared with such fury the desert shook, windows cracked in towns twenty miles away. Towers of flame hurled the ships skyward, their armored bodies tearing through the cloud cover. For a heartbeat, the night turned to day as three pillars of fire clawed into the stars.

In the control room, investors broke into applause, some weeping, others cheering.

Dier did not move. His eyes stayed locked on the screen, watching three blips streak into the void.

"Let them believe it can defy Earth," he said quietly. "In six months, I'll see a return on my invest-ment. Or they will vanish."

Space swallowed the Titans whole. Three armored transports cut silently through the black, their engines burning white-blue against the stars before fading to a steady glow. Inside, the men and women of Stavos's mercenary force strapped them-selves into their compartments, rows of steel boxes lined with screens and restraints. They stowed their rifles, so each cared for their own weapon.

The voyage to Mars was six months, but it wasn't life. It was endurance.

The cabins were dim and metallic, humming with the throb of reactors, the hiss of recycled air. The soldiers slept in shifts, their bunks stacked like morgue drawers, each one sealed behind sliding hatches. Meals were ration bars, thick and tasteless, swallowed more than chewed. Conversation was minimal, voices clipped and cold.

They weren't a family. They weren't comrades. They were weapons in storage.

Colonel Venn walked the narrow corridors, boots thudding against the deck. His men straightened automatically as he passed. He checked that their weapons were stowed, discipline solid, and posture straight. His voice was low and gravelly, the voice of a man who had broken armies before.

"Your bodies are tools. Keep them sharp. Sleep when told. Drill when told. Eat only enough to stay functional. Mars won't forgive weakness."

No one argued. No one complained.

In Titan-16, Major Helena Cross oversaw the psych teams. They sat at consoles, whispering into headsets, sending simulated feeds through drones, test runs of the voices they would unleash on Mars.

Commands disguised as familiar tones, desperate cries scripted to confuse, to erode trust.

Cross leaned against a bulkhead, cigarette smoldering between her lips, eyes narrowing as one feed played: "Aries Karalis... stand down. Your people are already lost."

She smirked faintly, exhaling smoke into the stale air. "By the time we land," she told her officers, "they won't know whose voice to trust."

ON TITAN-15, Captain Steele cackled as he prepped charges in the cargo bay. Explosives lined the walls, shaped, packed, polished to perfection. He ran his hand over a crate like a man caressing a lover.

"Once we crack their shells," he said to no one in particular, "we'll watch their domes fold like paper. And the sound when the air goes out..." He laughed, a sound too sharp, too wild.

A younger soldier shifted nervously. Steele grinned at him, teeth white in the dim light. "Don't flinch, kid. Fire is cleaner than mercy."

Lieutenant Holt sat alone, cross-legged in the barracks. He sharpened a blade, long and thin, its edge gleaming like ice. His squad drilled in silence behind him, moving in unison: disarming techniques, close-quarters stabs, strikes that killed in the width of a heartbeat.

Holt never raised his voice. He didn't need to. The men watched his movements, mirrored him, and became extensions of his will. When he finally spoke, it was quiet and flat.

"When the shooting stops, you finish the work. No hesitation."

In the command capsule of Titan-17, General Anton Stavos sat in his chair, broad shoulders motionless, eyes fixed on the forward displays. Mars glowed faintly in the distance, a red ember against the black.

His officers rotated shifts behind him, but Stavos did not sleep. His hands rested on his knees, his jaw locked tight. He was thinking not of the colony's farms, or its families, or the boy who wore his father's coat. He was thinking of an empire. Of obedience. Of fear.

The silence of space pressed heavily around him. His voice when he finally spoke was low and cold.

"Three ships," he murmured. "One mission. Mars belongs to Earth. Or it belongs to no one."

24

WEB OF MARS

The colony was no longer just a home. It was becoming a fortress.

Every day the hum of farming and building blended with the thrum of hammers and the clatter of scavenged parts. In the fields outside the domes, cadets and colonists sweated under the thin Martian sun, testing defenses one by one, not from blueprints or theories, but from the dirt itself.

The razor wire.

The first reels of wire were unspooled across the red plain, not strung tall like fences but laid low, grids stretched knee-high across shallow trenches.

Stephanie Delgado tugged at her helmet straps and frowned as she stepped gingerly over the test lines. "Doesn't seem like much," she muttered.

"Try dodging arrows as you cross it," Atlas grunted.

She gave him a look, then signaled a cadet to take a slow walk through the pattern. On cue, another cadet shoved him and then tossed a rock at him. — Not hard, just enough to cause him to step to the side. His boot snagged on the wire, and he heard a steady hiss. The suit's leg ballooned slightly where the line dug in, pressure hissing faintly before the safety alert sounded.

The boy scrambled upright, wide-eyed.

Atlas's lips curved into something like a smile. "That hiss? That's death on Mars. Doesn't need to kill 'em outright. Just make a hole. Mars does the rest."

The realization sank in. No bullets. No explosives. Just thin air and sharp wire.

Atlas duct taped the cadet's suit and told him to get back inside the colony.

AT THE FAR edge of the compound, Wright and Schmidt argued over resistance while cadets cranked the first catapult into firing position. The machine looked crude, welded together from structural beams, steel cabling, and spring drums.

"Won't work," Schmidt said, wiping sweat from his brow. "The torsion is too weak. Waste of time."

"Shut up and watch," Wright shot back.

The release lever snapped. The arm swung. A boulder launched into the pale sky, rising higher than any of them expected. For a breathless moment, it seemed weightless, drifting in a slow arc, then it slammed into the plain nearly a kilometer away, kicking up a plume of dust like a small explosion.

The silence broke into shouts and whistles.

SCHMIDT'S SCOWL cracked into a reluctant grin. "Lower gravity," he admitted. "Stone flies farther. Hits harder. Hmm."

Cadets were already rushing to reload, eyes wide with excitement.

SKYE GATHERED a group in the greenhouse commons with hastily strung iron bows. They laughed at first, fumbling arrows, teasing each other as they missed wide on the targets.

Then one cadet drew back, the string creaking, and loosed. The arrow cut clean across the air, slicing faster and farther than it had any right to. It slammed into a steel target and stuck deep, the shaft quivering.

The laughter died.

Skye walked forward, yanked the arrow free, and held it up. "No muzzle flash. No heat. No jam. Just speed and silence."

She notched it again and let it fly. Another strike. Dead center.

Aries felt a thrill in his chest. Bows, ancient Earth weapons, had found new teeth in Martian air.

In the wide corridor that opened to the outside, Holder oversaw the testing of the first fan array. The turbines groaned to life, blades slicing through the thin atmosphere. A roar filled the plain, and within seconds the sky turned blood-red, dust whipping into a storm that swallowed domes and people alike.

Cadets staggered, blind in the choking haze. Visibility dropped to arm's length.

Wright stumbled into Aries, coughing. "Can't see a damn thing!"

"Exactly," Aries said, pulling him upright. He could barely make out Rocky's lights blinking through the storm like fireflies. "They won't either."

· · ·

WHEN THE DUST SETTLED, the colonists gathered in the commons for the unveiling of Skye and Aries's newest creation. The weapon sat on a tripod, cobbled together from reactor coils, focusing lenses, and stripped comm arrays.

"It's not perfect," Skye warned. "It overheats fast. But it works."

She squeezed the trigger. A beam of light cut across the hall, shrieking as it scorched through a steel plate, leaving molten edges glowing red. Gasps filled the chamber.

Eleni shimmered at Aries's side, her voice calm and unsettlingly soft. "Light blinds. But resonance kills. A tuned frequency, calibrated to helmet glass, will shatter it. One breath of Mars...and they're gone."

The hall fell silent. The colonists looked at one another, wide-eyed.

"Doesn't take a bullet," Wright murmured. "It doesn't even take much power."

Aries looked across the crowd — the farmers with soil still under their nails, the engineers with grease-stained sleeves, the cadets with arrows slung across their backs. They weren't a militia. They weren't soldiers.

They were something Earth couldn't predict: Martians, armed with both the future and the past.

"We use what works," Aries said, his voice carrying over the silence. "Stone, wire, light, or sound. Mars is our ally and a weapon. And we'll use every inch of it to survive."

25

MUCH TO LOSE

The alarms didn't ring. There was no call to battle, no rush of soldiers. Instead, the colony was filled with softer sounds: the hurried shuffle of medics, the hiss of sterilizers, the muffled cries of Skye as she labored in the habitat's new medical wing.

Aries stood just beside her, his hands clasped hers. She squeezed so tight they ached. The corridors of Mars had never felt so narrow, the air never so thin. His heart beat harder than any launch or crisis had ever made it.

Dr. Klein's eyes softened above her mask. "It's a boy!"

Aries all but stumbled. Skye was pale with exhaustion, but her smile nearly knocked the air out of his chest. In her arms now, wrapped in a soft cloth spun in the textile wing, was a boy. Their boy.

"Your son," Skye whispered. Her voice cracked, her lips trembling as tears slid down her cheeks. "Aries... he's perfect."

The baby's fist curled tight around his mother's sleeve, then loosened to brush his face. Aries bent low, kissing the tiny hand, unable to stop the tears burning his own eyes. His whole world fit inside this moment — Skye, his son, the warmth of life blooming in a place meant only for death.

Outside, word spread like wildfire. Families gathered in the central commons, parents lifting children into their arms, cadets clapping each other's backs, older colonists smiling through tears. In every face there was awe, and in every heart, a new weight: something precious to lose.

Atlas lingered on the edge of it all, arms crossed, his expression unreadable. The grizzled veteran, who had buried too many comrades on too many worlds, found himself... unsteady.

Jamie Acosta, head botanist, stepped quietly to his side. She had soil on her sleeves, a leaf tangled in her curls. Without saying anything, she pressed a small sprig of green into his palm, a cutting of basil she'd been tending.

"For luck," she said softly.

Atlas turned the leaf in his scarred fingers. He couldn't remember the last time anyone had given him something fragile, something living. His throat closed up, and when he looked down at her, he saw not a botanist, not another colonist, but someone worth protecting.

"Jamie..." His voice came rough, unused to gentleness. He shook his head once, then bent, pressing his forehead briefly to hers, the closest thing to a vow he could make. For the first time in decades, Carl Atlas had something to fight for that wasn't survival. It was someone he cared about.

That night, under the glow of the colony's grand hall, Aries climbed the platform at the center. Skye sat nearby, their child cradled against her chest. The crowd hushed; hundreds of faces turned toward him.

Above them, the faint shimmer of orbiting ships cut across the Martian sky — Earth's fleet. Predators coming to strike.

Aries gripped the rail and let his voice carry.

"We all know what's coming," he began, his voice steady but low. "Three warships. Soldiers trained to kill. They think Mars is weak. They think we're fractured, afraid, still tethered to Earth."

He paused, letting his eyes sweep the crowd. Families huddled together, children clinging to their parents, lovers standing shoulder to shoulder, engineers still streaked with grease, botanists with dirt under their nails. People. Vulnerable. Precious.

"But look around you. We are not weak. We are alive. We've built more than a colony; we've built homes, farms, laughter, love. We've built a future that no one on Earth can give us, and they want to take it away."

He gestured to Skye, to the tiny bundle in her arms. "My son was born today. Another child of Mars. He's proof that we're more than survivors. We are creators. Builders. Families. We are a people now."

His voice rose, thunder echoing in the dome.

"Earth has nothing to offer us but chains. Out there, orbiting above us, they see us as an investment to protect or destroy. Down here? We see each other. We are the ones who plant, who mend, who guard, who dream. Mars is not theirs. Mars is ours. And we will fight for every child, every friend, every love. We fight for each other!"

The hall erupted. Cheers, stomps, hands pounding tables until the dome shook. Tears streaked faces, fists punched the air, the roar of conviction filling the habitat like a storm.

Atlas caught Jamie's hand, gripping it hard. Skye kissed their son's head, whispering words Aries couldn't hear. And Aries, standing tall in his father's coat, felt the truth thrum through him.

Mars had much to lose. And that made them stronger than any army Earth could send.

26

SKY FALLING

The warning came from the sky itself. Three fiery streaks ripped through the thin Martian atmosphere, contrails slashing across the pale red dawn. The Titans had arrived.

Aries stood atop the command gantry in the greenhouse ring, the whole colony spread out below him like a breathing organism, domes glowing, farms pulsing with light, drones buzzing in formation. His father's coat was regal as he raised his voice over the comms.

"They're here. Man your stations!"

The colonists manned their crude but massive siege engines, counterweights locked, baskets brimming with boulders wrapped in netting and steel scrap. The silence before impact was suffocating.

The Titan-15 flared its retro-thrusters, shaking the ground as it sought a gentle landing. Aries dropped his hand.

"Now!"

The catapults groaned and snapped forward, their payloads arcing impossibly high in the weak gravity. The first volley struck true, one missile of stone and steel slamming into the rocket's midsection. The Titan shuddered, lost balance, and toppled like a falling skyscraper, slamming into the regolith with an earth-shaking crash.

On the wall, Atlas let out a roar of laughter. "Try unloading artillery from that, you bastards!"

The second Titan-16 was still hovering, descending in careful bursts of flame. The catapults reloaded, counterweights slamming down, and another barrage arced upward. This time the great machine tilted, slammed side-first into the dust, and split its own landing struts. Two down.

But the third Titan-17 made it down clean. Its hatch hissed open, and out poured an army of Earth, fifty armored soldiers in matte black, their boots kicking up red dust. Behind them rolled three Humvees, each bristling with weapons, and two heavy artillery guns dragged on modular treads.

"Artillery crews!" General Stavos's voice barked over their comms. "Target those catapults. Fire at will!"

The first shells screamed out, their trails carving thin white scars against the salmon sky. They overshot by miles, disappearing into the horizon. Adjustments. Another volley, closer, but still well wide.

"Idiots," Atlas all but laughed.

Aries's lips curled into a grim smile. "I don't think they consulted their scientists."

The artillery teams recalibrated, aiming higher still. The third volley roared skyward, nearly vertical, before vanishing. Minutes passed. Then nothing. They had flung their rounds into orbit.

By the time panic spread through the Earth crews, the drones were upon them. Dusty led the swarm, smaller cousins buzzing around like angry hornets. They swooped down on the artillery, dropping explosive charges. The thin air turned rifles into furnaces. Their lubricants boiled away, their barrels glowing cherry-red after barely ten shots, jamming uselessly.

"Keep firing!" Stavos screamed, but his men were already slamming fists into locked bolts.

The Titan-17 came under fire just as suicide drones slammed into its landing struts, detonating in bright blossoms of flame. The rocket tipped, shuddered, and collapsed.

But the enemy's prize was still moving. A squad wrestled a heavy black case from the wreckage — their failsafe. The nuclear device. They loaded it onto a Humvee, the crate secured under armored clamps.

Stavos himself climbed into the passenger seat, his jaw clenched like iron. "Forward!" he bellowed. "We will finish this now!"

The column advanced.

The Martian defenses waited. Fans the size of wind turbines roared to life, kicking up vast sheets of dust. Visibility dropped to a few meters. Razor wire grids lay hidden beneath the red haze, knee-high tangles designed for one thing only: to tear holes in suits.

The first wave of soldiers stumbled into the trap. One fell, screaming as the knee of his suit split open to a vacuum. Another tripped, his glove torn. Within minutes, the atmosphere stole them. They convulsed, froze, and lay still, red dust already claiming their bodies.

Arrows whistled next. Simple shafts tipped with hardened steel. In Earth's atmosphere, they would have been toys. But here, in thin air and low gravity, they flew like bullets, piercing suits, releasing oxygen and heat. Each hit meant death.

The Humvees plowed ahead, but even their tires shredded on the hidden wire grids. Dust and confusion swallowed the battlefield. Stavos clung to the dashboard, barking orders into static-filled comms, but his army was in a quagmire.

The invaders had brought their war to Mars. And Mars itself was fighting back.

THE BATTLEFIELD WAS CHAOS, dust so thick it turned the world into blood-colored fog, shouts breaking into static over radios, the crack and hiss of failing rifles. Colonists ducked low behind berms, firing arrows into the storm, every shot meant to puncture a visor or joint seal.

Then came the panic. Desperate soldiers, blind in the haze, opened fire into the red wall. Bullets snapped and pinged through the air, striking steel, stone, and flesh. A cry cut out. One of Aries's cadets went down, clutching his side, his suit tearing as air streamed out like steam. Another colonist fell moments later, their chest plate shattered by random fire.

Atlas, seeing the chaotic death of his dear cadets, ran to man the resonance cannon.

From the platform above the choke point, the weapon ignited. A low, thrumming pulse rolled across the battlefield like the heartbeat of the planet itself. At first, it was just sound, a vibration deep in the chest, but then the effect bloomed. Helmets across the dust cloud spider-webbed with cracks, faint lines first, then shattering crescents. Soldiers gasped and scrambled, sealing breaches with gloved hands. Oxygen vented in sharp, white streams.

The scream of panic turned to retreat. Dozens stumbled backward, fleeing through the dust, dragging their wounded toward the broken shells of the Titans. The Martian air took the rest, silently, mercilessly.

But one voice still cut sharply through the storm.

"Advance, you cowards!" Stavos's voice tore through comms, ragged with fury. His Humvee roared forward, tires spitting red grit as it tore through the choke point. Behind him, the last loyal squads pressed on, grim and desperate.

Aries saw it, the armored crate mounted in the back of the vehicle, black and humming with silent menace. The nuclear device.

The Humvee rattled closer, unstoppable. Stavos himself leaned from the passenger seat, helmet flashing through the dust clouds. His hands moved quickly across the arming panel.

"General!" a soldier shouted. "It's suicide!"

"Then we finish this!" Stavos roared. His gloved hand smashed down on the activation switch. Warning lights flickered crimson across the crate, bathing the cab in a pulsing red glow.

And then, the energy lances struck. Directed beams from the colony towers slashed through the haze, white-hot lines carved into the Humvee's hood. The engine shrieked and died. Stavos's chest buckled under the blast. His helmet burst, shards glittering in the storm. He slumped sideways, dead before the Humvee ground to a halt.

But the nuke was still armed.

Aries's heart thundered. His mother's voice whispered urgently in his ear: "Critical activation sequence engaged. You have less than two minutes."

He didn't hesitate. He ran, boots pounding into the dust. Every breath felt too thin, too sharp in his chest. Colonists screamed warnings behind him, but he didn't stop.

The Humvee loomed ahead, black crate glowing red with its deadly countdown. The body of Stavos lay sprawled beside it, one hand still clutching the trigger assembly.

Aries vaulted onto the vehicle, ripping open the armored clamps. Heat seared his gloves. His mind raced faster than his fear, parsing wires, panels, protocols. The red digits blinked down: 1:19 ... 1:18 ... 1:17.

Next correct thing, he heard his father's voice echo in memory.

He bent over the panel and began to work.

The Humvee groaned under his boots as Aries yanked the hatch wide. Inside, the nuclear device pulsed like a heartbeat, its status panel alive with angry red numerals.

01:15 ... 01:14 ... 01:13

"Mom," Aries gasped, breath fogging inside his visor. "Talk to me."

Eleni's voice whispered in his ear, calm but urgent. "It's a Soviet-derived failsafe. Multi-sequence arming code. Four redundant loops. The trigger is armed at the hardware level."

Translation: there wasn't a neat little switch to flip. If he pulled the wrong line, it could detonate instantly.

"Great," Aries muttered, sweat dripping down his temple. His hands shook as he pulled open the side panel. A tangle of cables met him — red, yellow, black — each braided with shielding and heat insulation. His heart hammered so loudly it almost drowned out the countdown.

01:02 ... 01:01 ... 01:00

"Aries!" Skye's voice crackled in his comm. "Get out of there! It'll take you with it!"

He forced himself to breathe. "No. I can do this."

He remembered his father's voice, quiet but steady in the nights they trained together: "The next correct thing. Always focus on the next correct thing."

ARIES SHUT OUT THE VOICES, shut out the panic. He traced each wire in his mind, mapping it like the systems he'd rebuilt a hundred times over. He could almost see the flow of energy, the pathways humming with lethal intent.

His stylus was already in his hand, the sharp end flicked open. He jabbed it into the panel and forced a diagnostic loop. Eleni overlaid a schematic in his visor, ghost-lines flickering against reality.

00:47 … 00:46 … 00:45

"Four loops," he whispered. "Two fakes, one live, one redundancy."

He dug deeper, fingers flying, ripping away shielding. The device fought him, with a hiss of electricity arcing as he pulled a grounding clamp. Sparks jumped, stinging his glove. He hissed but didn't stop.

"Left conduit," Eleni murmured. "But be careful; the polarity is reversed."

He nodded, barely aware he was speaking aloud. "Reverse polarity… reroute feedback…"

00:32 … 00:31 … 00:30

He found the live line, a braided silver-black cable humming like it was alive. His chest constricted. Cut it wrong, and the device might believe it was under attack and detonate immediately.

He bit his lip so hard it bled. "Okay. Bypass first, then cut."

Hands trembling, he jammed the stylus into the secondary loop, bridging two nodes. The panel sparked, numbers flashing faster.

00:22 ... 00:21 ... 00:20

"Dammit, hold!" he shouted, sweat blinding him.

He slapped a palm over the bridging wire, forcing it to stay. Then, with his other hand, he yanked his multi-tool and sliced through the black cable.

A deafening hum filled the air. The countdown stuttered.

00:15 ... 00:14 ... 00:13 ... 00:12 ... 00:12 ... 00:12

The numbers froze. The glow shifted from red to amber. The nuke... was disarmed.

Aries collapsed against the crate, chest heaving, gloves shaking so hard he nearly dropped the tool.

For a long moment, there was only silence, the faint hiss of Martian wind through shattered plating.

Then Skye's voice, breaking with tears: "You did it. Aries, you actually did it."

ATLAS'S GROWL FOLLOWED, full of relief: "Damn kid, you saved us all."

Aries laughed then, a raw, broken laugh that felt

like sobbing. He pressed his helmet to the crate and whispered, "Next correct thing, Dad. I did the next correct thing."

BEHIND HIM, the colony stirred, cheers rising through the dust, families clutching one another. For one fragile heartbeat, Mars was theirs again.

27

ULTIMATUM

The battlefield was hushed, but it wasn't peaceful. The Martian wind blew faintly across the dust plains, stirring red fog around the dead and dying. The silence was broken only by the hiss of failing suits and the distant hum of the colony's fans winding down.

Aries stood on the Humvee, his father's coat hanging heavy on his shoulders, the disarmed nuclear crate glowing cold at his feet. His words had been spoken; now they lingered like smoke across the comm channels.

Fight and die in red dust or surrender and join us. The choice is yours, but it is as simple as live or die.

For a long moment, no one moved. Then, on the

mercenaries' private channel, voices broke out in jagged bursts of fear and anger.

"They're bluffing," one soldier growled, his tone sharp, panicked. "Earth won't abandon us. We're assets. They'll send another ship."

"They didn't tell us about the damn atmosphere or the gravity," another spat. "Rifles jam after ten shots. Lubricants boil off. Artillery fires into space! You call this a fight?"

"They're colonists," a younger voice cut in. "Farmers and kids. You really want to surrender to a boy?"

"Farmers?" a woman barked, bitter laughter crackling over her mic. "Did you not see what they just did? They toppled Titans like toys! They built weapons out of sound, for Christ's sake. They're more than kids; they're survivors."

The argument raged, voices overlapping until it was chaos. Some shouted for surrender; others swore vengeance. A sergeant tried to rally them: "We're soldiers! Professional! We don't bend to colonists..." but his words were drowned out by curses, pleas, and silence.

Back at the colony, every voice was audible. Eleni had patched the mercenaries' debate into the public channel. Colonists sat frozen in the mess hall, clustered around screens or clutching each other's arms. Families listened with wide eyes. Children leaned against their parents, sensing the weight in every word.

"They're fighting with each other," Skye whispered beside Aries, her voice just for him. Her hand trembled against the railing. "They don't know what to do."

Atlas, looming at Aries's side, gave a low grunt. "When your enemies fight each other, you should let them."

The colony murmured, some urging patience, some begging Aries to finish them now before they regrouped. Acosta clutched her hands together, muttering the rosary. Wright scowled, muttering about risk. Even Klein's sharp voice cracked with tension: "What if they try again?"

Aries raised his chin. His mother's AI flickered in his visor, a soft halo in the storm. "They are listening," Eleni said. "Speak again, or let silence decide for them."

He didn't repeat himself. He just stood there, tall as he could manage, waves of dust swirling in the thin wind, letting the choice weigh heavy on their hearts.

Finally, a soldier broke ranks. He stumbled

forward from the mercenary line, his weapon dropping into the dust. His voice came over open comms, shaky but resolute: "I surrender. Don't shoot."

Gasps rippled through the colonists. One of the cadets shouted, "They're coming!" and aimed a bow, but Aries lifted a hand.

"Hold fire. Let him through."

The man walked slowly, hands raised. His boots dragged over the razor wire grid, careful not to stumble. Colonists rushed to meet him, guiding him through with cautious hands.

Then another followed. Then two more. A small trickle broke from the mercenary mass, casting rifles aside, helmets turned toward the colony.

But not all.

Near the wreck of Titan-16, a knot of diehards clustered around a scarred sergeant Atilla Thrace, his visor streaked from an old wound. He lifted his rifle high and barked, voice thick with venom:

"Cowards! You'd kneel to a child? To farmers?" He spat the word like poison. "I'll die fighting before I bow to a boy!"

Several cheered, weapons raised in defiance. Their voices rose in a ragged chorus, the last embers of their pride clinging hard.

The colonists stiffened, fear and anger rippling

through the crowd. Some shouted for their deaths; others begged for restraint. Skye's hand gripped Aries's glove, hard. "Not all of them are going to listen," she whispered.

Aries's throat tightened, but he didn't look away. He saw it clearly now: two types of soldiers on the same battlefield, one crumbling under its own realization, seeing the inevitable, the others clinging to pride like a weapon.

"Then Mars will decide," he murmured.

Atlas's chuckle rumbled, cold and heavy. "Mars doesn't show much mercy."

"Let's leave them to it," Acosta said, nudging Atlas.

The lines were drawn, not by Earth, not by rank, but by choice. It' was theirs to make. Their weapons were jammed. All they had to do was seal the airlock and let the planet do what it did. Atlas nodded and walked with Aries towards the airlock.

With the dust having died down, the soldiers could see the colonists leaving the field along with twenty of their brothers in arms. Sergeant Thrace's blood grew hot. Cowardice and traitors kindled the rage further in his heart. He wiped a round, and his rifle and cycled the action several times. The soldier next to him realized what he was thinking and offered him his lip balm. The Sargent grinned a cruel smirk as he rubbed the wax over his gun's moving parts. He loaded the round and lay down to take aim.

The colonists disappeared through the airlock five at a time. Atlas and Aries waited to make sure the others made it safely inside. Aries looked over at the bodies of the fallen cadets. It hurt his heart. Mars was a brutal killer but took no joy in death. Those soldiers from Earth seemed to enjoy it. Those who surrendered were not the same as those still in the field waiting for their fate. Aries spoke softly to Atlas, I am glad it is over.

The words had barely left his lips when he felt a sting in his chest. He felt cold instantly as his vision narrowed. Through his visor, he saw Atlas collapsing next to him, and then it was dark.

"That's what I call a two for one," Thrace laughed.

28

WAR AND DEATH

The blood was small at first, like a red badge. Aries's chest hitched, shallow and ragged. He staggered, knees buckling, Atlas's massive frame crumpling next to him, helmet lights flashing red.

Acosta's laugh was lost to the pain she felt seeing Atlas and Aries fall through the glass of the airlock. Over the comm she yelled, "Help!! Aries and Atlas need help!" She cycled into the colony yelling for Dr. Kline.

"No!" Skye's scream cracked the comms, her anguish clear.

Out of the dust, Rocky walked and picked up Aries with one arm, and Atlas with the other, scooping him up like a child, and moved swiftly for the airlock. Dust swirled around his feet as he moved steadily forward. Shouts filled the comms with voices frantic and concerned.

"Dr. Klein! Aries is hit! He's hit!" Skye alerted the doctor.

The inner doors of the airlock opened, and colonists scrambled aside as Rocky barreled in, still cradling their limp bodies. Aries's suit hung loose, the fabric darkening where blood seeped through the hole.

Klein came running. "Get them on the tables now!" she barked. Her hands moved with frantic precision, cutting away suit layers, clamping tubing, fighting to stem the bleeding.

Atlas laid still, helmet still on, fists clenched. Skye couldn't stop pacing, couldn't stop looking at Aries's pale face. Her tech steady hands shook, the same hands that had dismantled and reassembled, now useless.

Atlas lay on the narrow table, his chest wrapped in clean bandages. Two medical cadets leaned over him, hands shaking as they checked vitals, their voices tumbling over each other in clipped medical jargon.

"Pulse dropping..."

"Stabilizer in, push another..."

"Clamp that vein..."

Jamie Acosta pressed herself against the side of the bed, one hand gripping Atlas's wrist as though sheer force might keep him alive. Her face was streaked with dust and tears.

"Don't you dare," she whispered, the words raw. "Don't you die on me.

One cadet glanced up, startled, but Jamie didn't care. She smoothed the hair back from Atlas's scarred forehead, her hands trembling. His eyes fluttered, unfocused, but the line on the monitor steadied.

"Pressure stabilizing," the senior cadet said with a sigh of relief. "He'll make it if he rests."

Jamie exhaled hard, a sound caught between a laugh and a sob. She bent close, her lips brushing his ear. "You stubborn bastard. I knew it would take much more to hurt you."

Atlas's lips twitched, barely a ghost of a smile, but it was enough.

They could see the table next to them, with medics shouting over the hum of equipment. And on it, Aries.

Jamie's breath caught. Aries's face was pale; his chest wrapped in crimson-soaked fabric.

Atlas stirred at the sound, forcing his head to

turn. His eyes widened, and the monitors jumped as he tried to sit up. "Aries…"

"Hold him down!" a cadet barked, pushing Atlas back against the cot.

Jamie's hands tightened around Atlas's, but her gaze locked on Aries's limp form. Her voice broke.

"God save him…"

The room shifted, every heartbeat, every breath, no longer about themselves but for the young man who had become the colony's heart.

"YOU CAN'T DIE, ARIES," Kline muttered under her breath, voice breaking. "Not after everything. Not like this."

The med bay's alarms screamed. Klein's voice was sharp, focused. "Pulse weak. Pressure dropping. He needs a transfusion and stabilization now!"

OUTSIDE THE AIRLOCK, pounding erupted — helmets, fists, boots slamming against steel.

Carter spun toward the sound, teeth bared. "Stay with them," he growled to Klein, then stomped toward the airlock. He slammed his hand against the control, and the cameras lit up, showing the figures outside: a half-dozen Earth soldiers, hands raised, weapons discarded, helmets streaked with dust and blood.

Their voices bled into comms, raw and desperate.

"Please! We're not with Thrace!" one cried.

"He's the one who fired! We tried to stop him!" another shouted, pounding the glass. "We slashed his suit. He's dead out there. We swear it!"

A third, trembling, fell to his knees. "We don't want to die. Please, let us in."

Carter's chest heaved with fury. His hands hovered over the lock release, then balled into fists again.

"You think I'll let you in?" he snarled into comms. His voice was angry, hoarse and hurt. "You shot Aries. You shot my friends. You shot our best chance of survival. If they die, you all die. Do you hear me? I'll watch the air leave your lungs."

The soldiers flinched at his words, one shaking his head violently. "It wasn't us! Thrace lost his mind. We tried to stop him, but he waxed his rifle, just to get a round off. He would've killed us too for wanting to surrender."

Carter's voice lowered to a growl, a wolf about to

tear flesh. "Mars doesn't forgive traitors. And neither do I."

Then, Eleni's voice cut in, soft and clear, the steady voice of reason: "What would Aries want?"

Carter froze. His jaw clenched. He saw Aries's pale face on the med table, his chest fluttering under Klein's hands. He saw the boy who had saved Mars with nothing but stubbornness and brilliance. The boy who forgave where others had only wanted vengeance.

Carter slammed his fist against the bulkhead, teeth grinding. Finally, he jabbed the release.

The airlock cycled, hissing open. The soldiers stumbled inside, gasping, grateful, faces lined with shock. After the pressure was balanced, they passed into the colony. Security's shadow fell over them like a reaper.

"You live for now," Carter growled, eyes like cold steel. "But hear me, if he dies, so do you. I'll walk you out myself and let Mars finish what it started."

None of them dared to speak.

Cambell motioned to the guards. "Lock them up. If they twitch wrong, you put them down."

As the soldiers were herded away, the officers turned back toward the med wing, where Dr. Klein worked feverishly under bright lights.

"Hold on, Aries," Schmidt whispered, voice breaking at last. "You don't get to leave us here alone."

ARIES DRIFTED IN DARKNESS. No pain, no dust, no weight pressing on his chest. Just stillness.

Then warmth.

He opened his eyes, or thought he did, and found himself standing in a place that could not exist. It was neither Mars nor Earth, but something in between. A meadow, soft and green, stretched under a sky that shimmered between blue and rust. The air smelled of blossoms and rain, the way his mother's garden had once smelled before the night she never came home.

"Aries."

The voice was a balm. He turned and there she was, Eleni. Not the AI projection he had built, not the fractured ghost of her in circuits and code. But his mother, whole and alive, her hair catching the sunlight, her smile soft as it had been when she tucked him in as a child.

He choked at the sight, his knees giving way. He sat there on his knees, crying. Tears streamed down his cheeks. "Mom..."

She opened her arms, and he fell into them, burying his face against her shoulder, trembling. The scent of her, the warmth of her, undid him. "I'm so sorry," he whispered. "You went out for me. You never came back because of me."

She drew back, cupping his face, her eyes shining but steady. "Oh, Aries. You didn't take me away. Love did. That was my choice, and I'd make it again; you are my everything."

He couldn't speak. The tears still ran hot down his cheeks, and she kissed them away. This was everything he needed. He had missed her so much. He just held her, becoming her little boy once again.

THEN ANOTHER VOICE, low and strong, rumbled behind him. "Son."

Aries turned. His father stood there, Commander Noah Karalis, tall in his uniform but softer now than Aries remembered him. The creases of worry and duty seemed lighter here. His eyes held no disappointment, only pride.

"Dad..." Aries's voice broke. "I wasn't there for her. I wasn't there for you. I keep failing..."

Noah stepped forward, laying a hand heavy and warm on his shoulder. "You didn't fail. You've carried more than anyone should have to, and you've done it with courage. I could not be more proud of you. You've done the next correct thing, time and time again. That's all I ever wanted for you."

Aries shook his head, lost between longing and guilt. "I'm so tired. I don't know if I can keep fighting. It feels like Mars just keeps taking from me."

Eleni stroked his cheek again, her voice soft. "Then you can rest. Stay with us. Here, there is no war, no hunger, no pain. Just love."

Noah's eyes locked with his. "Or you can go back. To your wife. To your son. To the colony that needs you. That choice is yours, Aries. No one will make it for you. We will always be here for you."

Aries's breath caught. Images flickered before him — Skye's face, fierce and tender all at once. The newborn, his son, was so impossibly small in her arms. The colony, their laughter at mealtimes, the hum of the greenhouse, Rocky and Dusty whirring like loyal companions.

"I DON'T WANT to leave you," Aries whispered. His voice trembled like a child's again.

Eleni said, pressing her forehead against his. "We are part of you. Always."

Noah squeezed his shoulder — firm, grounding. "I love you, my son."

This was everything that Aries had ever wanted — to be in his mother's arms feeling everything was going to be alright, and to hear his father's admiration and respect. He wanted this to last forever.

His mother kissed his brow. "I love you, my son. Stay in the light or go back to the fight."

Noah's hand tightened one last time. "Remember: the next correct thing. Always."

Aries closed his eyes, heart torn open with love and grief, and chose.

29

CHOOSE

The meadow shimmered. The air grew thin, the smell of blossoms fading into antiseptic and steel. Voices called his name, distant but insistent. Skye's sobbing plea, Atlas's rough growl, Klein's crisp commands.

The world returned in fragments. A soft hiss of oxygen. The rhythmic beeping of monitors. The sharp tang of antiseptic in the air.

Aries's eyelids fluttered, heavy as lead. For a moment he thought he was still in that meadow, that his mother would be there when he opened his eyes. Instead, light stabbed into him, clean and clinical, and pain lanced through his chest with every breath.

"Aries?"

Skye's voice was raw and trembling. He turned

his head with effort and saw her, eyes red-rimmed, hair plastered to her forehead from tears and sweat. She clutched his hand as if she was holding the world together with it.

"You're here," he rasped, voice so dry it was barely a sound.

"I never left," she whispered. Then the dam broke, tears streaming down her cheeks as she bent over him. "You scared the hell out of me."

He managed a ghost of a smile. "I saw my mother."

A shadow loomed, and then Atlas was there, broad as a wall, scar catching the light. His helmet was gone, and his face, usually carved from stone, was softer, almost broken.

"Damn kid," Carter muttered, and cleared his throat roughly. "You don't get to pull that stunt again."

Aries tried to laugh, but a cough came out. "Wasn't... my idea."

Dr. Klein swept in then, brisk and sharp as ever. "He's stable now, but weak. The round pierced his lung. We managed to repair the tear, but recovery will take time. He's alive because Rocky carried him fast."

Aries closed his eyes briefly, the weight of

exhaustion pulling at him. But behind his lids he didn't see the meadow anymore; he saw Skye, their child, the colony. The choice he had made.

"I saw my mother," Aries said to Skye.

Skye smiled at him, knowing how much his mom meant to him.

"Glad you are okay, Atlas," Aries said.

When he felt a little clearer, his voice was steadier. "How many surrendered?"

Skye squeezed his hand, reluctant to answer. "Some. Enough. They're locked up." Carter said, "... if you didn't make it, they wouldn't either."

Schmidt's jaw flexed. "Solid plan."

ARIES SHOOK HIS HEAD WEAKLY. "No. If they surrender, they live. That's the next correct thing."

Carter's eyes darkened, but after a long moment, he nodded. "You're too much like your old man, that means thirty-two new settlers," he muttered.

Aries's lips twitched. "I'll take that as a compliment. I saw my father too."

THE MONITORS BEEPED STEADILY and strongly now.

Klein fussed with the IV line, but her voice softened as she spoke to him. "Rest. You've earned it."

But Aries's gaze stayed on Skye. Her hand in his was warm, trembling, but real. Their son's photo — one of the cadets must've brought it — was propped on the table beside the bed. The tiny face looked back at him, fragile and new.

He swallowed hard. "I chose to come back," he whispered to her. "For you. For him. For all of us."

Skye leaned down and pressed her forehead to his, tears damp against his skin. "Then don't you ever leave again."

For the first time since the shot, Aries closed his eyes not to drift away, but to rest. And this time, he wasn't afraid of waking.

THE MAIN HALL had been transformed. Once a plain room for dining, it now bore a cement platform at the far end, poured and smoothed by Schmidt's crew. At its center stood a great chair made from Martian dust — not elegant, but strong, solid stone. A throne.

Aries walked slowly down the center of the hall, every step a reminder of the wound that still ached in his chest. His father's coat hung over his shoulders, patched and stained, big still but worn like armor. Skye walked at his side, steadying him with the lightest touch of her hand. Behind them, Atlas's heavy boots echoed like drumbeats as he guided Jamie. He still looked weak but was healing.

The colony had gathered, all of them. Families filled the long tables, cadets lined the walls, system officers stood shoulder to shoulder. Even the surrendered Earth soldiers were there in a line, their helmets set aside, their faces drawn but resolute.

When Aries reached the platform, a murmur rose through the crowd. Then voices, louder, insistent.

"Sit!" someone cried. "Sit, Commander!"

"Sit, Aries!"

"The throne is yours!"

He shook his head, heart hammering. "I'm no king," he said, voice raw. "I'm just..."

Atlas's hand pressed firmly between his shoulder blades, urging him forward. "Sit," the old soldier growled. "You've earned it."

Skye smiled softly through tears. "This is theirs as much as yours. Let them have this."

With a breath that felt like surrender, Aries lowered himself into the cement chair. It was cold and rough against his back, imperfect, unfinished, just like the colony. Just like him.

The hall erupted. Cadets cheered, officers clapped, families rose to their feet. The surrendered soldiers, one by one, accepted their king, bowing their heads. Each voice rang out as they pledged, the sound carrying like a tide:

"I pledge loyalty to Aries Karalis."

"I pledge loyalty to the colony."

"I pledge to Mars."

Atlas's voice was heard above them all. "Long live Aries the First!" And every Martian saluted their king.

Then came the chant. It started small, a ripple of voices, then swelled until the air vibrated with it.

"Aries the First! Aries the First! The King of Mars!"

The words echoed against the steel and cement, shaking the hall like thunder. Children stamped their feet in rhythm, cadets pounded their fists on tables, the sound becoming a single heartbeat for the colony.

Aries's chest tightened. He wanted to argue, to deny it, but as he looked out at them, he saw hope in their eyes. They weren't just cheering for him. They were cheering for themselves, for survival, for the world they were building together.

He raised a hand, and the hall fell quiet. His voice cracked but carried.

"I'm no king," he said. "But I will be whatever you need me to be. I will keep us alive. I will keep us thriving. And I will never, ever, stop fighting for Mars to be our home."

The roar that answered him nearly shook the walls.

"Aries the First! The King of Mars!"

He sat on the throne, heart aching with humility and fear, but also with pride. His father's words whispered in his mind: The next correct thing.

And for now, the next correct thing was to accept the crown they had already placed upon his shoulders.

30

NUKED

The council chamber was dim, the only light being the glow of the holographic map. At its center hovered Earth and Mars, the void between them traced by thin white lines marking past launches. Aries stood with his arms folded, Atlas to his right, Skye to his left. Around them, the systems officers leaned in close.

"They'll never stop," Aries said, voice low but steady. "So long as they think we're alive, Earth will send more soldiers, more Titans, more death. They don't see a colony. They see property."

Acosta leaned forward, her hands stained with soil. "So, what then? We hide?"

"Not hide," Aries said, eyes hard. "Disappear."

The plan was brutal in its simplicity. Carter had

designed the circuitry; Cambell had adjusted the capacitors; Schmidt had overseen the construction. A pulse emitter, cobbled together from salvaged Titan cores and colony-built capacitors, capable of unleashing a burst strong enough to mimic the electromagnetic signature of a nuclear detonation.

It would not kill. It would not do any harm. But Earth would believe Mars had died in fire.

The landing site was barren, scarred by the wrecks of the fallen Titans. Dust hissed across the plain, whispering through jagged metal. The colonists had hauled the emitter piece by piece, Rocky and Dusty dragging the final coils into place.

The machine stood like a crude altar, its coils humming, the red sky reflected in its steel.

Aries placed his hand on the activation panel. His chest still ached from the wound, every breath a reminder of how close he had come to death. But his mind was clear.

"This is how we survive," he said quietly. "Not by fighting them again and again, but by making them believe Mars is gone."

Atlas nodded, grim satisfaction on his scarred face. "Let the bastards choke on their own lies."

Skye reached for Aries's hand, squeezing it once before he pressed the switch.

The pulse tore across the plain in a bloom of invisible fire. Dust lifted in a great wave, rocks shuddered, the wreckage of the Titans sparked and went dark. Above the thin sky, instruments screamed and satellites blinked out, blinded by the burst.

To any eye watching from afar, it was unmistakable: the death throes of a nuclear blast. And then, silence.

ON EARTH, the Mars Expedition Control Room erupted in chaos.

"Massive energy spike, unmistakable nuclear signature!"

"We've lost telemetry! All channels dead!"

"Confirming... nothing. Mars is silent."

Director Caulder was gone, but the new regime, hired generals and accountants in pressed suits, stared at the data with growing horror.

"They detonated it," one whispered. "The colony... it's gone."

"Years of investment," another snarled. "Billions. Wiped out."

A third slammed a hand against the console. "Shut it down. Liquidate everything. Salvage what we can from patents and tech. The Mars project is over."

In less than an hour, the feeds were cut. The investors fled. The company dissolved. Earth turned its eyes elsewhere, chasing new profits, and Mars, red and silent, was forgotten.

ATLAS FOUND Jamie Acosta in the greenhouse after dinner. She was kneeling by a row of bean plants, brushing soil from her palms. The scent of damp earth filled the air, almost enough to make him forget the dust outside.

He stood there for a long moment, awkward, helmet under his arm, the words chewing at him like gravel. Finally, he cleared his throat.

"Jamie... I don't know how to say this," Atlas rumbled. His voice was low, almost rough. "I don't know how to love someone. I don't even know how to... be with someone. I've spent my life breaking things, killing people, taking orders. That's all I've ever been good at."

Jamie rose slowly, brushing dirt from her knees. She studied him with her head tilted, eyes gentle but unflinching.

"Atlas," she said softly, "you think I know what

I'm doing? I've loved plants my whole life, not people. I don't know how to be a partner, or a wife, or anything else. I've always been better with roots than with hearts."

For a moment, silence hung between them, broken only by the hum of the grow lights. Then Atlas let out a rough laugh, shaking his head.

"We make a fine pair then," he muttered.

Jamie smiled, uncertain but warm. She stepped closer, close enough for him to smell the faint sweetness of basil on her hands. He bent down, clumsy, unsure, and she lifted her chin. Their kiss was awkward, hesitant, almost colliding, but honest.

When they pulled back, Jamie chuckled nervously. "Well. That wasn't graceful."

"No," Atlas admitted, his scarred mouth twitching into a grin. "But maybe we'll get better at it."

She touched his hand, fingers light, and for the first time in years, Atlas didn't feel like a weapon. He felt... human.

In the new observation lounge, Aries sat with Skye. The room was vast compared to the cramped halls of the first habitat, its wall a broad pane of reinforced glass. Beyond it, the Martian horizon stretched forever, the sky painted in pale golds and bruised reds as the sun slid down.

THEIR NEWBORN SON lay in Skye's arms, small and warm, a fragile heartbeat against the infinite silence of the planet.

Aries leaned closer, brushing a finger against the boy's tiny hand. The baby's fist curled tight around him. His throat tightened.

"I love that he is Martian," Aries whispered. "Not from Earth. From here. From Mars."

Skye rested her head against his shoulder, her voice soft. "What should we call him?"

Aries watched the sun dip lower, the shadows stretching across red stone. His father's words echoed faintly in his mind: Do the next correct thing. His mother's AI had told him once that life was about more than survival; it was about choosing to build.

"Aries the Second," he said at last. His voice was steady, almost reverent. "Not because I deserve it. Because he will. He'll carry the name into a future that belongs to him, not to Earth."

Skye smiled, her eyes shining in the last light of day. "Then Aries the Second it is."

Together, they sat in silence, the three of them, watching the Martian sunset burn and fade. Behind them, in the heart of the colony, families laughed, children played, and voices carried through cement halls filled with green life.

"No one's coming," Skye said softly.

"No one," Aries agreed. His hand lingered on hers. "Mars is ours now."

Atlas and Jamie joined Aries and Skye in the observation room. Skye noted the cute way they held each other's hands.

"So, this is a thing?" Skye asked, smiling at the deep red color of Atlas's face.

"We are figuring it out," Jamie replied.

Atlas crossed his arms, staring at the horizon. "So... what do we build, King of Mars?"

Aries looked toward the domes glowing faint in the distance, toward the farms, the children, the families. His people.

"Everything," he said.

Mars was no longer just about survival.

It was home.

AUTHORS NOTE:

The question of whether we would leave Earth for Mars has always fascinated me. In my classroom, I discovered the answer was a powerful reflection of human nature. We'd start with the facts, the blueprints from NASA and SpaceX—but the spark always came from the story of Alyssa Carson, a young woman preparing for that very journey, whose ambition made the impossible feel real.

Then, I'd ask: "Would you go?" The answers were a mix of pragmatism and poetry. Many clung to Earth, citing the lack of internet, the immense dangers, or the unbearable loss of saying a final goodbye to everyone they loved. They saw what would be left behind.

But a few saw only what lay ahead. They were explorers, dreamers who weren't deterred by the risk. Their eyes lit up with the vision of being the first to build a home on a lifeless planet. They are the inspiration for this book.

This story is born from that spirit of exploration, a spirit first ignited in me by the tales of authors like Edgar Rice Burroughs and Andy Weir and fueled by the breathtaking images sent back by rovers on the Martian surface.

Thank you for joining the journey in Aries I - The King of Mars. The adventure continues in the sequel, Aries I - Children of the Red Dust, which chronicles the colony's struggle to expand amidst a new uprising. I hope to share it with you next year.

Jeremy D Scholz

www.ingramcontent.com/pod-product-compliance
Lightning Source LLC
Chambersburg PA
CBHW020700110726
47901CB00001B/258